This Book Has Been Donated by
The McDougal Foundation, Inc.
a Maryland Nonprofit Corp.

# CRACKDOWN IN
# THE BOTTOMS

# CRACKDOWN IN
# THE BOTTOMS

Stephen DeVore

Hope Publishing

This is a story based upon actual events. The author has changed the names, characters, and places in order to protect the privacy of the innocent and to prevent the guilty from gloating over the facts.

Crackdown in The Bottoms. Copyright © 2002 by Stephen DeVore. All rights reserved. Printed in the United States of America. No part of this book may be used or reproduced in any manner whatsoever without written permission except in the case of brief quotations embodied in critical articles or reviews. For information, address Hope Publishing, P.O. Box 65423, West Des Moines, Iowa 50265.

Scripture taken from the HOLY BIBLE, NEW INTERNATIONAL Version. Copyright © 1973, 1978, 1984, by International Bible Society. Used by permission of Zondervan Publishing House. All rights reserved.

Library of Congress Control Number: 2002102908

ISBN 0-9718710-0-0

First Publication

Published in the United States

1 3 5 7 9 10 8 6 4 2

Hope Publishing

This book is dedicated to my children.

Several months after the birth of my first child, a daughter, I clearly remember telling her mother that I had reservations about having a second child. I questioned if I could love another child as much as I had grown to love my daughter.

Two years later, my son was born. I quickly learned that there was enough love in my heart to love my son as much as I loved my daughter.

The only thing that has remained constant in my life has been the love that I have for my children.

# Introduction

This is a true story about two men and how them meeting one another changed both of their lives forever.

I was an undercover detective with a college education and sixteen years of law enforcement experience. Other than one speeding ticket, I had no criminal history.

The other man was also educated. But his education came from the streets. When we met, he lived in an area of Indianapolis known as the Bottoms. And unlike me, he had a criminal history. It began with a 1956 arrest in Florida for attempted burglary and possession of burglary tools. Since then, he had also been arrested and charged in four other states with forgery, carrying a concealed weapon, armed robbery, violation of the national firearms act, robbery, conspiracy, being a fugitive from justice, and carrying weapons.

It is clear to see that we had lead entirely different lives prior to our meeting. As you read this story, you will learn that we both made choices that would dramatically change our lives forever. We made our choices based upon obtaining and keeping our earthly treasures. You will see what our treasures were and what finally happened to them.

# Chapter 1

Nate, age six, one of my two stepsons, was anxiously anticipating the annual Fun Night at his elementary school. He had made plans to meet one of his classmates in the gym. After supper, Nate was the first one dressed. He tried to be helpful by getting his three-year-old brother dressed. However, Joel did not want any help on this particular night. Nate attempted to bribe Joel by telling him that he would give him two of his tickets if he would hurry up. While that didn't speed things up, we eventually found ourselves in the car and ready to go.

Westwood Elementary School in Indianapolis was full of children dragging their parents from room to room. Each classroom offered a different game to play. We tossed rolls of toilet paper through hanging toilet seats, knocked over plastic bowling pins with dodge balls, and tried to win a cake in the cakewalk. The next game that the boys were interested in was guessing how fast they could throw a baseball. Nate had his eye on winning a New York Yankees helmet.

As Nate stepped up to the pitcher's line, my pager started to vibrate. My wife, Paula, had become accustomed to my pager going off at any given time during the day or night. I understood that it took a special person to be married to a detective, especially an undercover detective. As I reached for my pager, I could only guess who it might be. It could have been the sergeant, dispatch, an informant, or perhaps one of the county attorneys working late. Most of the pages that I received needed to be returned promptly. It didn't matter if I was at home relaxing or out with my family. The job I chose did not have set hours.

I saw the page was from the county sheriff's office. I told my wife I hoped to return shortly. She knew that when I answered a page there was no guarantee that I would be gone for only a short period of time. So when she smiled and said, "Yes, but hurry," I sensed that she was not pleased with the timing of the page. As I hurried off to find the closest phone, my pager vibrated again. The message was a duplicate of the first page, "Please call dispatch right away."

I stepped into the principal's office and returned the call. Paul, one of our evening dispatchers, answered the phone on the first ring, "Riverside County Sheriff's Office." One of our road deputies, Jim, had contacted Paul and requested that a narcotics officer call him at home right away.

Jim had been working in the sheriff's office for about twenty years. I liked Jim. I could always count on him if an incident turned ugly and a backup was needed. If Jim was getting involved in something while he was off-duty, I guessed that his call must be important. Some of the younger deputies seemed to call constantly, wishing to pass along information. They had aspirations of one day working undercover and hoped that their information would be the foundation for an important case. I knew how it was because at one time I had been in the same position. I hoped that I would never lose that rookie drive to crack the "big one." I loved going to work each and every day.

Ever since high school, I had dreamed about being a detective and working undercover. After I graduated from college I started my career in law enforcement. Many of my friends had been shocked that I wanted to pin on a badge and strap a gun to my side. I was quiet, reserved, and I avoided confrontations. Even though I was an all-conference football player in high school and had accepted a football scholarship to attend college, my friends did not see me as a person who would get involved in a dispute. I had never been in a fight, and I didn't have a practice of raising my voice. But after taking a law enforcement class during my senior year in high school, I knew what I wanted to do with the rest of my life. And I wasn't just interested in being a uniformed officer. I wanted to be a detective.

After fourteen years in the uniformed division, I finally realized my dream. The day that I was promoted to the organized crime unit was one of my proudest days. Even though my pager would sometimes wake me up at 3 a.m. or I would get calls while I was out with my family, I had no regrets. I had waited a long time to have the opportunity to work undercover. Few police officers ever get the chance to have such an assignment. I vowed to always work as hard as I did on the day I was promoted. I realized that there was a fine line between being dedicated and being obsessed. I hoped that I would never cross that line and that I would never lose the balance that kept my priorities in order.

I found a pen, wrote down Jim's phone number, and dialed it. When Jim answered, he apologized for calling me after work but he insisted that I needed to speak with his neighbor, who was at his house and was upset. Jim said that she wanted to speak with a detective. I explained to Jim that I was out with my family but I would talk with her briefly. I felt that since it had been important enough for her to stop by Jim's house to pass along information, I would take the time to listen to her concerns. As a detective, I needed the public's assistance. I always made it a practice to return pages to informants and concerned citizens. It might have been one of the reasons I experienced a good rapport with informants.

As Jim handed the phone to his neighbor, I could hear the woman crying. I immediately knew that it wasn't going to be a brief call. The crying woman introduced herself as Alice and pleaded for my assistance. She explained that she was tired of seeing drugs ruin the lives of so many people. She asked me if I had heard about the young woman who had been shot in the face several days before on the south side of town. Alice insisted that the young woman was a friend of hers. She said she could not sit by and allow the violence that was associated with drugs to continue. Her crying intensified so much that I found it difficult to understand her. I tried to reassure her that I would do my best to help her and her friend. I had learned early in my law enforcement career that it was best not to make promises to people. Instead, I always offered them hope.

I spent the next several minutes trying to calm her down and reassure her that I would meet with her in person the following morning. Alice insisted that she would do whatever it took to bring down the man who was responsible for operating the drug house where her friend had been shot.

Fifteen minutes had elapsed since I first returned the page. I thanked Jim for calling me and asked him to take down the primary information on the alleged drug dealer and forward it to me the next day. As I hung up the phone, I wondered if the information might lead to the big case I had been waiting for or if it was just an over inflated story told by someone who meant well.

I hurried back to my wife and saw Nate wearing a New York Yankees batting helmet. He had correctly guessed his final throw at 23 m.p.h. I was disappointed to have missed his throws. But at the same time, I was wondering what would happen during my meeting with Alice the next day. I congratulated Nate on his prize, and we continued to enjoy the Fun Night. Unfortunately, we didn't win a cake in the cakewalk. By the time we used our last ticket, it was nearly 8:30 p.m. I had no idea at the time just how much that one page would change the rest of my life or the lives of so many others.

After we got the boys cleaned up and tucked into bed, Paula asked me why I was gone for so long following the page. Some of my colleagues chose not to share their work experiences with their spouses. However, I found that it helped to relieve the stress I experienced on the job. I also felt that it would help Paula understand me better. I found her to be very objective, and occasionally our conversations helped me see things I might have overlooked. I told her about Alice's concerns and her willingness to get involved in the investigation. I told her how Alice had referred to the drug dealer as one of the biggest and most dangerous drug dealers in Indianapolis.

When I first started working as a detective, I believed each informant when he or she would describe a person as being a very big drug dealer. Each time I debriefed the informant about the quantities of drugs the dealer sold, I felt it would truly be the big case I had been waiting for. But as each case unfolded, the dealer inevitably turned out to be a small-level distributor.

It was difficult being a rookie and watching the senior detectives assigned to cases that were, as I call them, gimmes. They didn't have to work very hard at these cases, and the end results were always large quantities of drugs seized and piles of money forfeited.

I hoped that in time I, too, would have an investigation that would have significant results. I wanted to believe an informant when he or she spoke of large amounts of drugs and cash. So, with some reservation, I told Paula that Alice had said that the drug dealer went by the street name of the Godfather.

I explained to Paula that I had seen the news report about the woman who had been shot in the face. Having worked in law enforcement for so many years, I tended to associate a shooting with either a domestic dispute or a drug deal. The incident had taken place in a part of Indianapolis known as the Bottoms. The neighborhood was old and run-down. The people living there had very little money. The area was racially diverse.

In the news clip I saw, a reporter had interviewed the owner of the home where the shooting had occurred. The homeowner was a White male who appeared to be about fifty-five years old. He was thin, had a receding hairline, and spoke as if he were uneducated.

His yard was unkempt and cluttered with junk cars. Several old campers were scattered about the property. In fact, the shooting had allegedly occurred in one of the occupied campers.

I told Paula that after considering what Alice had said about the Godfather's drug operation, I wondered if the shooting was, in fact, drug related. I quickly dismissed the thought and assumed my newest informant was simply another concerned citizen exaggerating the facts. However, I couldn't help considering the possibilities. What if the information Alice had given me was true?

Paula was a very good listener. I had often shared with her the same type of story and information. She always listened intently as if she had never heard it before. This time I saw the concern in her eyes when I told her about the shooting. She knew that if given the opportunity, I would attempt to get an introduction to the Godfather in an undercover capacity. I knew that the best case that an officer could present to a prosecutor was one involving an undercover hand-to-hand buy from a drug dealer.

Having lived in the Chicago area, Paula was familiar with the violence associated with the drug culture. She viewed these deaths differently than the people who only saw them on the big screen or simply read about them in the newspaper. For her, violent, crime-related deaths were real life, not a movie. I was her husband; I wasn't an actor with a stunt double.

Paula did not want to lose me to a drug dealer's bullet. Because she had lost her mother to cancer and her oldest brother in an auto accident, Paula knew what it felt like to lose someone close to her. So when I shared tragic events with her, she asked me to be careful. I could hear the concern in her voice. She also said that if there were anyone who could take down the Godfather, it would be me.

The following day, I started my shift with the usual morning meeting. At the meeting, we would brief the sergeant about our plans for the day. It was also a time to share intelligence information.

After Joe and David, it was my turn. I started by telling everyone about the conversation that I had had with Alice the night before. I told them that she had provided information about a person she knew as the Godfather. I was careful not to build him up in case he turned out to be an average drug dealer. She had said that he lived in the Bottoms and had a variety of people living in his house and in campers on his property. I told them that she had warned me that the Godfather and his people had guns.

I caught Stuart's eye as I was repeating some of her accusations. He seemed to be unusually interested in what I was saying. Finally, he interrupted me. He said that he had received information about the same person two months ago. I had apparently been off on the day he had briefed the unit. Stuart went on to say that the Godfather was the individual who had been interviewed on the news several days ago about a shooting that had occurred on his property. Stuart's information indicated that the people on the property were selling drugs – crack, cocaine, and methamphetamine – for the Godfather. It didn't surprise him when I said that Alice had claimed that there were a lot of guns on the property.

Stuart also said that he had examined some garbage removed from the Godfather's property on pickup day, but had run into a dead end and had discontinued his investigation.

Stuart told me that he still had several items from the Godfather's garbage in his office. Following the meeting, Stuart showed them to me. I found a few items to be particularly interesting. There was a picture of a man dressed in prison clothes with a note written on the back saying, "To Robert from Lenny." The second item was a business card stating:

>Your Satisfaction Our Guarantee.
>Dancers - Models - Entertainers -
>In call - Parties - Outcall and Escort Services
>We do it all.

From my experience with vice investigations, I knew that the card was an advertisement for prostitution. Two Indianapolis phone numbers were listed on the card, but no address. The third item was a letter addressed to 1000 S.E. Lexington, which was the address of the garbage collection. And finally, the most important piece of evidence was a large plastic bag.

Because that type of packaging is commonly used by drug dealers to hold large quantities of drugs, it would seem to indicate that the Godfather could be distributing drugs.

I asked David, the detective who handled the drug-sniffing dog, to have his dog make a run past the plastic bag. He agreed, and instructed me to hide the bag in one of my desk drawers. Next, he brought in the dog and proceeded to lead him over and around various objects.

The dog showed no interest in the bookshelf, trashcan, or my gym bag. But he barked and scratched at the drawer in my desk where I had hidden the plastic bag, indicating he'd detected the presence of drug residue.

That's when I decided to start building a case against the Godfather, as I had yet to see a low-level drug dealer store small amounts of drugs in such a large plastic bag. Could it be that the information Stuart and I had received was correct?

At that time, I was training a rookie detective, Tracy. She had been in our unit for only a short period of time and was doing a great job. Tracy, who had previously worked in the patrol division, was the first woman detective to work undercover in our unit.

I called Alice and asked if Tracy and I could meet with her right away. She said she could be ready in thirty minutes. She gave me her address and directions to her home. Normally, we didn't meet an informant at his or her home especially on the first meeting. Officer safety was the primary reason. Another reason was to ensure that people were not attempting to learn our identity by having their friends lure us into their homes, then simply say that they had changed their minds. But in Alice's case, I felt comfortable meeting her at her home because she was Jim's neighbor.

Tracy and I loaded up the items that we needed to sign up a prospective informant: a Polaroid camera, fingerprint pad, and a five-page, confidential, personal history form.

About forty-five minutes later, we arrived at Alice's home. It was a small one-story house with paint peeling away from the siding and gutters coming loose from the roof. The gate on the backyard fence was open. Several old cars sat in the yard. Most were on jacks with the tires missing and one was without an engine hood. There were also a variety of other junk items, including an old washer and dryer. I hesitated to think what the inside of her house might look like. As we approached her front door, I read a posted sign on the porch: "Beware of Dog." When I knocked on the door, I could hear several dogs barking.

A White woman who appeared to be about forty-five years old came to the door. Her hair was short, dirty, and unkempt. She was wearing an old, faded, pink sweat suit and tattered white tennis shoes that had several holes in them. She was about 4 feet 10 inches tall and weighed about 150 pounds.

I'll never forget the smile she had on her face. She greeted us as if we were her closest friends. She quickly invited us into her home. I introduced Tracy and myself. She told us that her name was Alice and her friends called her Al. When I thanked Alice for calling us, she interrupted me and insisted that I call her Al.

As we started talking, I glanced around the living room. Her furniture was old and worn-out. Dirty plates sat on the coffee table and three bulldogs were milling around the room. The room smelled of dog waste, cheap perfume, and cigarette smoke. If all of that wasn't bad enough, the furnace must have been set at eighty degrees. I could only hope that the time we were about to spend in that environment would prove to be profitable.

Al moved one of the bulldogs off the couch and asked us to sit down. She launched into her story, telling us that she had known the Godfather for many years. She admitted that her deceased father had been a fence, buying and selling stolen goods. She had become acquainted with many thieves and criminals as a result of her dad's business dealings. I asked her if she knew the Godfather's real name. She told us that his name was Robert Porter. And then, without warning, Al started to cry.

She said that it was very hard for her to snitch on the Godfather because he was one of her closest friends, almost like a father to her. For years he had taken care of her when food was scarce or she needed to borrow money. Many times Al had been unable to pay him back. She said that he was a kind person, someone who would take in people off the street and give them a place to stay until they could get back on their feet.

I told her that I was confused. The night before on the phone, she had described him as a dangerous man, one of Indianapolis' biggest drug dealers. Why was she portraying him as a candidate for citizen of the year? She stopped crying, glared at me, and said, "Someone has got to stop him." During the past year, she claimed, the Godfather had gotten her hooked on crack. Because of her drug abuse, she and her husband were barely speaking. And when they did, they argued.

Then she asked me if she could get into trouble for what she had been doing to repay the Godfather for the money and drugs that he had given her. I sat quietly for a minute, wondering what she had done, then encouraged her to explain. Al confessed that she had been helping the Godfather manage his outcall, or prostitution, service.

She picked up a spiral notebook and handed it to me. As I read through it, she explained how the service worked. She said the Godfather had installed a second phone line in her home and that she would answer it during set hours. She said that the line had been disconnected following the shooting on the Godfather's property because he'd said that he wanted to lay low for a while. The number to her second line was one of the two numbers listed on the business card that Stuart had found in the garbage at 1000 S.E. Lexington, the Godfather's house.

Al went on to explain that each of the girls was listed in the notebook by a street name, but she could identify each one of them. In the notebook, she recorded the time that she received a call, the customer's first name, the girl that the customer wanted, how long the girl was at the hotel or house, and how much the girl was paid. Al was supposed to receive a small percentage of the money earned. At times, Al was asked to drive the girls to the hotels or houses. She said that sometimes the Godfather would find out where the customer lived. If the customer appeared to have money, the Godfather would send several of his people over to the customer's house and burglarize it while the customer was at the hotel. Other times they would simply rob him at the hotel.

Al said that the prostitution business was becoming too violent. As evidence, she said she believed that the Godfather had been involved in a recent homicide. I remembered the incident that she was referring to. She explained that the Godfather had hated the man who had been murdered because some of the Godfather's prostitutes had switched alliances and had been working for the other man. The Godfather was outraged and feared he was losing control of his business. She said that he had had some of his people rob the other man and beat him to death. It was meant to send a message to everyone not to mess with the Godfather.

The murder had occurred in August 1994. The victim, Gary Patterson, was found on the bathroom floor of his mobile home. He had been bound, gagged, and severely beaten. Patterson lived on the south side of Indianapolis, near the Bottoms.

Al went on to say that the Godfather had also gotten involved in the drug business. She thought that the most recent shooting on the Godfather's property had been drug related. She said that the victim of the shooting, Amanda, was a very good friend of hers. It was the final straw as far as Al was concerned. Al said Amanda had been living with the man who shot her. Al described Amanda's boyfriend as a nut who always carried a gun and was not afraid to use it.

She said that the Godfather used the people living on his property as security for his drug business and to solicit customers. She said that he was the only one permitted to sell drugs on his property. She indicated that there was only one entrance to his house, and he kept it locked at all times. She said she heard the Godfather say, more than once, "The reason I lock the doors is to buy time in case the police raid my house."

Many times a man would stand guard at the door after a person entered the house. Al told us how people were assigned to look out the second-story windows and watch for cops. Others were responsible for patrolling the property around the house. At night, they used night-vision glasses.

She described how the Godfather had installed surveillance cameras to detect anyone who approached his residence. The monitor was in his office so that he would know instantly if there were trouble.

I asked Al to explain how the organization was structured. She said the Godfather was the head of the prostitution and drug operations and estimated that his organization consisted of twenty-five to thirty people. She said that he started selling drugs every day about mid-morning and continued until midnight. It was a hard-and-fast rule that the doors were locked at midnight and that no customers were allowed in after that, though he did occasionally make exceptions for his valued customers.

Al said that the drug sales routinely took place in the privacy of his office. She said that the Godfather carried either a silver Smith & Wesson 9mm handgun or a .380 automatic handgun when he was selling drugs. The Godfather also owned shotguns, rifles, AK-47 assault rifles, and Uzis. She said that he would often accept guns as payment for drugs. Al said that every gun in his possession was always loaded and ready to be used to protect what was his.

There was a code in place to screen drug customers when they called. The Godfather also had hired a person to sweep the phone line to determine if the police had tapped into it.

Anna was next in the organizational hierarchy. Al described her as a White, twenty-year-old, former stripper whom the Godfather had taken under his wing. She said that he had been married to another woman when he asked Anna (who was seventeen years old at the time) to move in with him. After a while, the Godfather's wife moved out and Anna took over her role.

Al thought that the Godfather and his wife had never gotten divorced. Al said that Anna would help package the drugs, collect money from the customers, and take the drugs to the Godfather's office for the customers to purchase. She said that Anna carried a .380 handgun with her at all times.

She said Marcus, a Black man, was the Godfather's right-hand man. She believed that Marcus was the person who had taught the Godfather how to take powder cocaine and cook it into crack. She thought the Godfather used Marcus's connections to buy drugs from, then sell them back to, the Black people in inner-city Indianapolis. Al said that once Marcus and the Godfather started making crack, they quickly went from selling eight balls (an eighth of an ounce) of crack a day for $250 to selling a quarter pound of crack a day for several thousands of dollars.

Al said that Marcus was at the Godfather's house every day overseeing the daily operations and heading up the security force. If the Godfather needed to talk with somebody about his or her drug debt, Marcus would be the one that he would ask to go out and find the person.

Al thought that Marcus was coaching the Godfather as to who it was okay to sell to, how much to give them on credit, and, when there was a line of customers, who should be served first. Al stated that Marcus had a reputation on the street as a person not to be messed with. In order to have a successful drug organization, a person like Marcus was essential. She frequently saw Marcus carrying a handgun. Al said that he was not afraid to use it if he thought that it was necessary.

Al named some of the other big players in the Godfather's organization. She talked about Reggie, the forty-year-old White male who had shot her friend in the face. She said that Reggie always carried a gun (a .45 caliber semiautomatic, a .22 caliber handgun, or a .357 magnum revolver.) His main duty was to patrol the property. Al said that he sold glass smoking pipes that he made in his camper, which was parked on the Godfather's property.

Reggie also sold marijuana on the side. She said that it was a no-no, but nobody wanted to tell the Godfather. Personally, Al thought the Godfather probably knew about it and actually made a cut from the sales.

The next person Al talked about was Van, an Asian man in his late twenties. She said that he mainly provided inside security, either watching the front door or from the windows on the second floor. She described Van as a wannabee drug dealer who was not very successful. Van occasionally brought some of his friends to the Godfather's house to buy drugs. Van carried a handgun from time to time even though the Godfather did not trust him with one.

Another man who regularly served as a security person was Marcus's cousin Dwayne. She thought that he was about the same age as Marcus. His duties were both inside and outside security. Al saw Dwayne frequently carrying a .38 caliber handgun in the waistband of his pants.

Al said that some of the prostitutes who lived with the Godfather from time to time also served as lookouts including, Yvonne, Marcus's girlfriend and Maria.

I later learned that Maria was the driver of a car that was involved in a high-speed chase resulting in the death of an innocent person. Maria said that she was fleeing from an alleged pimp, who later was convicted of two homicides.

Al gave us the names of three boosters, or shoplifters, who traded their stolen goods for drugs. Al also provided the names and descriptions of other people who bought drugs from the Godfather and of those who sold drugs for him. The one thing that made Al's claim about the amount of drugs he was selling believable was the racial diversity of the Godfather's customers. They were Black, White, Asian, and Hispanic. I had never heard of a market as diverse as the one that he had apparently developed.

I knew that Al was giving us a lot of valuable information about the Godfather. If even half of the information was found to be accurate, it had the potential to be the foundation for one of the biggest cases in our unit's history. The problem with many investigations was taking the information that was collected and actually putting it to use. It isn't as easy as it might appear. Police officers can't go out and arrest a person on information alone.

Even with the cooperation of informants, it is difficult to convince a jury of twelve people that a defendant is guilty beyond a reasonable doubt. It is even harder in the federal court system because of the mandatory minimum sentencing guidelines. Federal sentences for drug dealing are very harsh. For many jurors, it is difficult to find a person guilty when he or she would be facing ten years, twenty years, or even life in prison for conspiracy to distribute narcotics.

All that Al had to say about the organization captivated me, but I needed some fresh air. I knew that my clothes were going to reek. I looked at Tracy and asked her if she thought we had enough information.

She said, "Yes." The expression on her face indicated that she, too, was ready for some fresh air.

Tracy thanked Al for her time. Al took a sip from her thirty-two-ounce plastic cup of Pepsi and smiled.

I asked Al if she would help us in our investigation of the Godfather and his organization. Al replied that she would help in anyway she could. She started to cry again. She said that she had been involved with drugs and prostitution for far too long and had ignored too many things. She could no longer live with herself knowing what she knew. She said she knew that many people would get hurt or killed if she did not step forward.

I asked her if she would help me infiltrate his organization in an undercover capacity.

She replied, "I'll do better than that. I will introduce you to the Godfather himself."

# Chapter 2

As we drove away from Al's house, I looked back and saw her waving good-bye. I turned to Tracy and asked if she thought that Al was telling the truth about the Godfather and his organization.

"If half of what she's told us is correct, he is one bad ass drug dealer," Tracy said.

I told her that what amazed me was the diversity of the Godfather's customers. I joked, "He is definitely an equal-opportunity drug dealer."

We drove back to the office to tell the sergeant about our meeting with Al. Along the way, I commented that apparently Al was too busy to clean her house. Tracy replied that if we had stayed there too much longer, she was going to ask Al if she could be excused so she could go outside to smoke a cigarette.

I said, "I'm sure Al would have suggested that you went ahead and smoked as we talked."

Tracy laughed and agreed, saying that she probably would have bummed one from her and joined in.

I explained to Tracy that people who broke away from drug rings did so for a variety of reasons. They were sometimes in debt to the dealer and could no longer buy drugs from him or her. By cooperating with the police, they would erase their drug debt. Others wanted to eliminate the competition and start up a drug business of their own. I also explained that some informants came to the police with information because they were in the midst of arguments with ex-spouses and wanted to retaliate. In most of those cases, the couples would get back together and the assistance would end abruptly. Those informants tended to give very thorough information without embellishing the facts.

Tracy asked me which of the examples I thought Al fit. I was honest and said that I didn't know. Al appeared to be in debt for her crack addiction. But, the Godfather's terms of fronting crack to Al without pursuing her debt made me discount that motive. Tracy, however, reminded me that we were only hearing Al's side and that maybe the Godfather saw her debt differently.

I agreed. My last informant had forgotten to add a zero when he explained that he owed $1,800 for a past marijuana purchase. Later, while listening to the suspected dealer over an electronic listening device that the informant was wearing, I found out that he actually owed the dealer $18,000. It was a far cry from the $1,800 that we were prepared to pay in order to gain the informant's assistance in buying three pounds of methamphetamine.

While sexual relationships were a common way of getting drugs without spending money, Al was not the prettiest woman I had ever seen. I couldn't or didn't want to picture her as ever having been intimate with the Godfather. I had seen many attractive women who had become addicted to drugs establish sexual relationships with ugly, dirty men just to keep their supply of drugs flowing. But this didn't seem like the situation with Al, so I crossed that option off my list.

And it didn't seem to me that Al was hoping to go into business for herself. I knew I couldn't tell how intelligent a person was by his or her appearance, but Al didn't seem to be educated. In our initial interview she didn't strike me as a person who was capable of balancing her assets and liabilities. But then again, a person didn't need brains to be a criminal, and I had misjudged informants before.

"The street criminal is smart in his or her own way," Tracy reminded me.

I just couldn't think of a reason why Al would want to cooperate with us. Maybe she was attempting to learn what we knew about the Godfather and what information we already had on him. If that was her motive, she sure was playing her role well. She hadn't asked me a lot of questions, however.

Tracy suggested that Al might simply be fed up with the drugs and the prostitution. And after her friend was shot at the Godfather's house, she felt compelled to come forward. I agreed. Maybe Al was ready to break away from the lifestyle she had been living. Like any other addiction, giving up a life in the fast lane would be difficult especially since that was how she had lived for so many years. My only hope was that she would see it through to the end without falling back into the lonely, dark world of drugs and prostitution.

Al had talked briefly about a church near her house that she had started to attend. She said that she had become very close to the pastor. He was the only person she had told about her decision to come forward and help the police. The pastor had encouraged her to break away from her past. By helping the police in their investigation of the Godfather, Al would be giving something back to the community and it would be atonement for her actions. Because of my Christian faith, I thought Al's newfound faith would be her greatest asset. It would be the strength she needed to break the spell that the Godfather and the drugs had on her.

When I looked at the clock in the car, I was surprised that it was already 1:20 p.m. I had not expected to be at Al's house that long. It had been the most interesting debriefing I had ever done. My pager vibrated. I was to call the sergeant in his office right away.

The sergeant demanded perfection. As a result, our unit was highly respected by state and federal agencies. I had a great deal of respect for his abilities as a detective.

As we got closer to the office, Tracy suggested that we stop at a fast-food restaurant and grab something to eat. We drove through the nearest one and headed back to the office. As we drove, I warned Tracy I intended to minimize what Al had told us. Then if it turned out to be accurate information, we would have exceeded his expectations. And if the case did not progress, the sergeant could not find fault with how we conducted the investigation.

After quickly eating our lunch, Tracy and I went to the sergeant's office and briefed him. I kept it simple. The only obstacle was answering why it took so long.

When I concluded, he said, "You have a lot of work to get done before you have a case here."

Sometimes an investigation comes together about as easily as trying to put a puzzle together in the dark. If only it could be as easy in real life as it appears to be on television. We had a lot of work to do before we could take advantage of Al's willingness to help.

I was fortunate to be training Tracy at the time. In most case investigations, we worked by ourselves. This time I would have help, and Tracy was very eager to get to work.

Our first task in investigating the Godfather was to identify him. I called the power company to find out who was registered for service at his residence, 1000 S.E. Lexington. Velma, the representative I spoke with, told me that the power at that address was in the name of Della Porter. Velma also gave me Della's social security number. I asked her what Della had listed as her employment. Velma said that Della had indicated she was self-employed.

I laughed and said, "Why does that not surprise me?"

When people filled out their power application, it was not uncommon for them to list themselves as self-employed. One time I asked Velma to check the small print to see if the person had mistakenly filled out the truth and listed drug dealer. She laughed and after that, it was an inside joke when Velma read off their reported employment.

Next I checked with the phone company to see who had phone service at that address. I wasn't surprised to find out that two phone lines were listed under R.R. Fisher. I explained to Tracy that it was common for a person to list their utility service under another person's name. The same was true with their car titles and home mortgages. I guessed that the criminals' way of thinking was that if their property was not listed in their names, law enforcement officials could not seize their ill-gotten gains. It takes time but a good financial investigator is always able to follow the paper trail back to the suspected violator.

We decided to learn more about the person named R.R. Fisher. Maybe the Godfather's name was not Robert Porter. Maybe it was Robert Fisher. We checked with the Indiana Department of Transportation Drivers License Station. We found out that no R.R. Fisher existed with that name or with a date of birth close to what Al had given us.

I suggested that we drive by the Godfather's house and try to get the license plate numbers of the cars parked there. Tracy and I had not seen the house yet and wanted to see it firsthand. We were both very curious.

As we got close, I noticed that the house was one of three on a dead-end gravel road that was full of potholes. At the end of the road, there was an old path that led to a pallet business. We couldn't drive down his road without drawing attention to ourselves. We went ahead anyway.

The only visible address was on the mailbox. I wasn't able to see a name on the box. The house was an old, two-story, wood-frame residence. It was several different colors and it looked like a variety of siding materials had been used. It appeared as if an addition had been built onto the back of the house. Several of the windows were odd shapes and appeared to have come from a mobile home. I was only able to see one door. It was located at the back of the house along the gravel drive.

Al had said that the drugs were sometimes kept in the garage or somewhere in the backyard. She also told us about a tent near the garage where a person would sleep occasionally. Al thought the Godfather had one of his security people sleep in the garage to protect the cash and drugs. The oversize, one-car garage had a sliding wooden door. It appeared to have a lock on it just as Al had described.

As we got closer to the house, I could not believe how many old trucks and cars were parked near or on the property. We counted a total of eleven of them parked on both sides of the street, in the driveway, and in the yard. We also counted three campers in the yard. We were only able to write down a couple of the license plate numbers.

Most people imagined that all big drug dealers drove expensive cars and lived in large, beautiful houses. The Godfather, it appeared, lived in a rundown old house in a bad neighborhood with old beat-up cars and trucks cluttering his property. I told Tracy that it was common practice for a drug dealer to take a person's car when he or she was in debt to him. Over the years, I had seen many situations where a drug dealer's property looked more like a used-car lot than a home.

There was a large dog chained up next to the garage. During the previous couple of years, we had run into more and more drug dealers who were training and using dogs for security. Just by looking at the size of the dog, I didn't think he needed training to perform security duties. His size alone would have stopped me from getting near the house.

From our observations, we thought it was quite possible that the Godfather was maintaining a sizable security force on his property. There was only one streetlight on the dead-end road, so the area was probably very dark at night. While Tracy and I saw only two men outside of the house when we drove past, we knew that we could be detected. There were a significant number of places on his property (the garage, the campers, the house, and the tent) for people to keep watch from. I felt sure that we were being watched as we drove past the Godfather's house.

That night after putting the boys to sleep, I shared the day's events with Paula. She sat attentively as I told her about my meeting with Al. She was interested in what I had to share with her. I hadn't intended to tell her so much. But I would no sooner finish one sentence and another interesting thing would come to mind. I tried to minimize anything that might cause her to worry unnecessarily. At this point in the investigation, I was merely relying on one person's information. I saw no reason for her to be concerned about the Godfather or about anything that could turn out to be unfounded.

Paula sensed that I was holding something back from her, even though we had been talking for more that an hour and a half. She said that she enjoyed hearing about my day and didn't want to put a damper on my enthusiasm. But she expressed a concern that the case involved prostitution. That was the one part of my job that she disliked, and she didn't hesitate to tell me. I understood her feelings. It was one thing for me to negotiate a drug purchase. But for me to be around women who would sell their bodies for whatever they could get, that was another story.

# Chapter 3

I first learned about Paula's feelings concerning prostitution when I told her about my first undercover experience. Shortly after receiving my promotion to the organized crime unit, I was asked to assist in a vice investigation into violations at strip clubs. The majority of the assaults that we were called to investigate occurred in the strip clubs, which were located just outside the city limits. Very seldom did a weekend go by when the sheriff's office wasn't called to handle a disturbance at one of the clubs.

When fights broke out, they were rarely conventional, with two men squaring off like boxers. Frequently, two or more men would jump a man while he walked to his car. Sometimes during a fistfight, one person would pull a buck knife from his pants and stab another person. We'd seen fights involving pool sticks, beer bottles, chairs, and even a toilet seat. The clientele that frequented the clubs came from all over central Indiana and was shady, at best. The men had several objectives: drinking, taking drugs, fighting, and of course, watching women strip while performing lewd acts of entertainment.

According to Indiana state law, the dancers were required to keep their nipples covered. Several members of the community had complained that violations were taking place at the local strip clubs. It was my assignment to pair up with another detective and investigate the reported violations.

As I got ready for my first undercover assignment, I thought to myself, *Why would a person who frequented such an establishment complain when the dancers removed their clothes? They weren't there for the food!*

I was nervous when the unit members met to discuss our objective. I was the only one who had not participated in an undercover vice investigation before. Everyone else appeared to be relaxed and looking forward to that night's assignment. Ron was joking about the first time that Greg had worked on a vice investigation. Apparently Ron had told the dancer that Greg was celebrating his birthday, so the woman directed her attention to Greg. I glanced over at Greg as Ron continued to tell the story for all of us to hear. Greg was turning bright red.

I had learned that the dancers were motivated by money. When they singled out men and performed for them, they expected to be tipped for their efforts. Many of the men who visited the clubs for the first time were honored to be given so much attention. They didn't realize that the women were simply performing for the crowd and were expecting the men to slip money into their G-strings.

The dancer had removed Greg's glasses and slipped them down the front of her outfit. She then motioned for Greg to remove them. He was caught off guard by her request and didn't know what to do. Should he follow her instructions or was it a violation of department policy? Ron had urged him to go along with her. Reluctantly, Greg did.

Then she danced directly in front of him while she played with her G-string. Greg did not realize that she was requesting a tip. After a moment of embarrassment, Greg took a dollar from his wallet and placed it in her G-string. He had quickly learned about the hazards of sitting in the front row, a lesson I would remember.

The sergeant split us up into teams. He assigned David and me to the Cage Lounge. I was feeling excited about my first undercover assignment, but was uncomfortable that it was taking place in a strip joint. I did not like the crowds that frequented those establishments. What if someone recognized me from when I worked in the uniformed division? I had thought that my undercover work would involve buying stolen goods, drugs, or hot cars, so I was not mentally prepared for what I was about to do. My experience with strip clubs was limited to professional visits, such as reports of fighting. I was not sure how to act or what to expect. David said that he would guide me through it. That's what I was afraid of. How would I react if a dancer singled me out and started to perform with me as her victim? Would the guys in the unit set me up as the birthday boy?

We were each given ten dollars and instructed to buy no more than two drinks. At 10:30 p.m., the sergeant wanted us to return to the office and write our reports. Because I was the new guy, David said that I would write the report.

David said that he would drive. He told me to get into his car and to put my badge in the glove compartment. David also reminded me to take the handcuff key off my key ring. If for some reason I took my keys out of my pocket, I would not want someone to spot the key.

On the way to the bar, I confessed to David that I was a little nervous about our assignment. I was not sure how he would react, but I wanted to be honest with him. He looked at me and smiled. He told me that he didn't like to work undercover in strip clubs either. I wasn't sure if he was being sincere or if he was baiting me.

We decided that when we got there we would split up the dancers. I would take the first and third dancers. He would take the second and fourth. Then when we sat down to write our report, it would be more accurate and more detailed.

For our report, Abby, an investigator with the Planning and Zoning Commissioner's Office, had asked us to make note of each dancer's age, race, height, weight, hair color, eye color, stage name, and legal name. Finding out a dancer's legal name would be a real test of our undercover skills.

Abby also asked us to keep track of what clothes a dancer was wearing, when she started her performance and what items of clothing she removed while she was stripping. We were asked to make note of any tattoos that a dancer might have. She explained that if any charges were filed, our detailed reports would help to identify the dancers. Many of the dancers traveled around the Midwest and were regulars at the clubs. In addition, Abby asked us to keep an eye on the waitresses to see if they were acting inappropriately.

We had to have our reports turned into Abby by the following day. Abby would take care of filing any criminal charges. We would only be called to testify if the matter went to court.

We walked into the bar. A bouncer checked my driver's license. I glanced around the large open room to see if I recognized anyone. The men in the room did not take their eyes off the woman who was performing on the stage. I was used to having people take notice of me as I entered a room because I was used to wearing a uniform. Tonight, even though I was working undercover, I still felt like a uniformed officer.

The club was full of smoke that hung from the ceiling. The place reeked of alcohol. It was the smell of beer that had been spilled and never cleaned up. The lighting was dim. There were green-and-red-colored spotlights focused on the woman who was dancing. She was on a raised platform that was approximately seven feet by seven feet. The dance floor was made of cheap tile. Around the edge of the stage there was a one-foot high railing that was covered with carpet. A shiny chrome pole was in one corner of the stage. The dancer was lifting her leg above her head and resting her heel on the pole.

David spotted an empty booth in the far corner. Shortly after sitting down, the waitress came to our table. She took our order and left without saying much. The music was loud and we were sitting under a speaker, so we could hardly hear each other. Most of the customers weren't talking, so the loud music didn't bother them. We felt like we needed to be careful about who was near our table when we discussed our assignment.

I felt like I had "cop" written across my forehead. I was waiting for the waitress to announce to the crowd that the vice cops were there. Shortly after we received our beers, one of the dancers who was working the crowd came to our table. Instantly, my blood pressure shot up. I felt a rush of warmth race through my veins. I'm guessing some of the customers experience that same rush. Their reaction, however, comes from the excitement of watching the dancers disrobe. Mine was from nervousness. What was I supposed to say to her? How was I supposed to act? I decided to wait for David to make the first move.

Apparently, she had just finished her dance set and was working her way through the crowd. The dancers made the majority of their tips that way. They would ask if they could sit on the customers' laps. What followed was up to each customer.

This dancer was a tall, slender, small-busted White woman who looked barely eighteen years old. She had on a see-through robe and no bra. Her G-string was bright red and full of one-dollar bills.

I looked at David for direction. He was staring at me in complete panic. His hands were shaking as he played with his beer bottle. He shifted in his seat. I thought that he looked more nervous than I was feeling. When the dancer asked us how we were doing, David just sat there looking at his beer. I looked up at her smiling face thinking, *I guess I'm on my own*. At that point, I realized with some relief that David wasn't going to set me up for a prank that would be shared with everyone during the debriefing. Sweat was beginning to form on his forehead. What was I going to do? When I tried to talk, I got a lump in my throat. I had had a similar feeling in junior high when I had asked Laura to slow dance with me for the first time.

The dancer moved closer and opened her robe to expose her breasts, which were in violation of the code – her nipples weren't covered! Panic gripped me. What was I supposed to do? It was not as if she was robbing me at gunpoint, but that was how I reacted.

The only word that I could force out was "Hi." How profound! My actions were those of a sixteen year old and not of a thirty-five year old. By now, I was convinced that we had given ourselves up as two rookie vice cops. We were busted. David continued to stare at his bottle of beer.

The dancer remained standing directly at my side, waiting for me to say more. It was apparent that she was getting impatient with me. With a half smile, she asked, "Are you working?"

What did she mean by that? Was she insinuating that we were vice cops on duty? Finally, David looked up at her and started to speak. He told her that we had just come from a business meeting and we were waiting for several more of our coworkers to arrive.

She asked if we wanted her to sit down and talk with us. I thought that David had relaxed and was going to take control of the situation. So, I waited for him to answer. Instead, he glared back at me as if to say it was my turn to do the talking. Once again, my mind went blank. I was unable to think of anything to say. Seconds of silence seemed like minutes.

I wondered what was going through her mind as she watched us sitting there like little boys. After some hesitation, I explained that I had just gotten married and it would be best if I didn't take her up on her offer. Once again, David was more interested in his beer bottle than he was in helping me get out of that situation. The smile left her face. She shrugged her shoulders in disgust and walked away.

When she was gone, it felt like the weight of the world had been lifted off my shoulders. I could not remember the last time I had felt like such a complete failure. Even though David had not acted any more convincingly, it didn't matter. I knew I was the rookie but I was still disappointed with the way I fell flat on my face. My mind had gone blank, and I was unable to think quickly on my feet.

How would I respond during an undercover drug buy? Or what would I say if a person questioned my cover story and accused me of being a cop? If I couldn't talk to a dancer who only wanted a couple dollars from me, I was sure to fail. The stakes would be much higher in an attempted drug buy because the consequences would be more severe. And I had another police officer next to me! Had I waited all those years to work undercover only to discover that I did not have what it took?

David didn't seem to want to talk about it, so I didn't say anything. I thought that maybe we were both embarrassed by our performances and were acting as if nothing had happened. We watched the other dancers a little longer and left.

As we drove back to the office for the debriefing, I couldn't stop thinking about the woman standing in front of me and my inability to function. What did it mean? I wanted to work as an undercover detective and infiltrate drug organizations. I didn't want to sit on the sidelines watching other officers as they worked undercover.

Was it simply a case of rookie jitters or was it a job that I was not cut out to perform? Was my illustrious career as an undercover detective over before it started? I did not want to be in that situation again.

By the time the Godfather case landed on my lap, I had become much more confident as an undercover officer. Since that night in the strip club, I had taken part in more than a hundred undercover assignments. I had learned the art of working undercover.

After listening to my wife's concerns about the Godfather case, I promised her that I would redirect the investigation if the focus ever centered on prostitution. I felt confident that I would be successful without having to put any undercover officer, including myself, in the "heat of the kitchen."

Paula reminded me that the *Indianapolis Register* had reported on an investigation concerning the allegations of misconduct by dancers at several of the local strip clubs. The reporter who attended the trial had written an article that included the names of the undercover officers and their testimony. In the article, which had been written prior to the Godfather case, the reporter also had described what the dancers had done to the undercover officers. After reading the article, many people came away with a misunderstanding of the officers' actions. What was reported, however, was different from what they had described during their testimony. No matter, Paula did not want to have the parents of the children who attended the day-care center that she managed read an article about her husband and any sexual activities that he may or may not have been involved in.

After telling her how I thought the Godfather investigation would proceed, she felt much better about it. My marriage was more important to me than putting criminals behind bars. There would always be people choosing to break the law, but there were very few women as wonderful as Paula. If I had to choose, I would choose to have a good relationship with Paula rather than trying to arrest a criminal at the expense of Paula's feelings.

# Chapter 4

Paula needed to be at work early, so the sound of the alarm clock woke me up at 6 a.m. I got out of bed and woke up the boys. Joel got up right away. Nate, however, took after his mother and was not a morning person. Finally, after three reminders, he made it out of bed. That day he had a spelling test, so I worked with him on his words while he got dressed. Joel wanted help with his socks. As was typical for Joel, it was easier for him to ask me for assistance than it was for him to try to get dressed by himself.

The boys were hungry. They each had two bowls of cereal. After breakfast, I offered Joel a treat if he would put his shoes on without asking for help. While Joel was busy doing that, Nate and I finished his spelling words. Nate was a bright student, but found it difficult to focus on schoolwork early in the morning. Because he was concentrating and was willing to work on his spelling and because Joel managed his shoes on his own, I gave them each a treat.

Paula came downstairs and thanked me for filling her water bottle. Then, like a flash, all three were out the door and off to day care. Even though it was still early, I got dressed and drove into work. I was anxious to get back to the Godfather's case. The sky was clear and sunny. I had a good feeling about what the day might bring. I felt fortunate to have a job that I really enjoyed. For me, it wasn't work. Instead, it was an adventure that offered something new and exciting every day.

At the office, I sat down at the computer and continued to search for information about Robert Porter. In order to complete the required paperwork, I needed a thorough and accurate description of the suspected drug dealer. I would either have to delay the purposed undercover buy from the Godfather until I could learn more about his identity, or I would need to fill out the paperwork using the limited information that I already had.

It had been my experience that informants started out with good intentions, but soon would get sidetracked and stop helping with the investigations. Their willingness to snitch on other people eroded when they had too much time to sit and think about their decisions. If they were not pressed into action immediately, they tended to drift away. Then we would lose the opportunity to tie together the intelligence information we had already collected about a suspected criminal with the information we were receiving from an informant. When combined, those two ingredients made an excellent case, a case strong enough to be presented to a prosecutor for the consideration of filing charges against a suspect.

I was worried that if I did not act on Al's willingness to help me infiltrate the Godfather's organization immediately, she would be like so many other informants and get cold feet and slip back into the lifestyle she was trying to escape. I had a hunch that Al would be able to do great things for us if the situation were handled correctly. One of the most upsetting experiences for an investigator was the mismanagement of an informant. It was like dropping a football that had been thrown for the winning touchdown.

After careful consideration, I decided to stop researching Robert Porter and fill out the buy sheet, which is the form that contains identifying information about a suspected drug dealer. Prior to the sergeant approving an undercover drug buy, the buy sheet had to be completely filled out. While the information that I had on the Godfather was not as accurate or as thorough as I would have liked it to be, it was enough to complete the buy sheet.

Once the unit's morning meeting was completed, Tracy and I drove to the south side to meet with Al. I called Al from the car and asked her to meet us in a church parking lot, which was within walking distance from her home. Al agreed. The neutral meeting place would serve two purposes. It would give us time alone with Al in case her husband had returned home. It would also spare us from having to sit in her smelly, unkempt living room. Al said that it was the church she attended, and she wanted to talk with her pastor anyway.

Traffic was light, so we arrived at the church ten minutes early. The church was in a quiet neighborhood. The parking lot faced the street, and the church building was at the far end of the lot. It was a well-kept, older building. There was a new sign that listed the pastor's name and the schedule of worship services. I parked next to an old paneled van that sat at the edge of the lot. There were two other cars parked in the lot next to each other. Based on the appearance of the three vehicles, the church membership was probably made up of people with lower incomes.

A few minutes later, Tracy noticed Al and an older, white-haired gentleman coming out of the church. Al was on time, which was uncommon for informants. Many of them had no reason to keep track of time. They stayed up late at night and slept until midday, just like a teenager on summer break.

Al saw us and waved. She had a big smile on her face. She grabbed the man's hand and they walked toward us. I guessed correctly, as it turned out, that Al was going to introduce us to her pastor. I could see how proud she was as she approached the car. Her actions reminded me of a child dragging her parents over to meet her new best friends.

The pastor seemed to be a little apprehensive. He stood slightly behind Al as she introduced him to Tracy and me. Al was quick to point out that we were her new friends and that we were going to help the community by taking drugs off the streets of Indianapolis. What a powerful statement!

Al continued to explain to him that we were the two people that she had been talking about. She told her pastor that she was going to help me infiltrate the Godfather's organization. She said she realized that becoming a police informant meant burning a lot of bridges and that it would be difficult for her to return to a life of drugs and prostitution. Al had obviously spent a lot of time thinking about the consequences of getting involved with the police before she made her initial call.

The pastor was reserved. I wasn't sure if he trusted us. He seemed to be relating to us as if we were stereotypical undercover detectives, similar to the ones he might have seen on television.

Al asked her pastor if he wanted to see our badges. He stepped toward the car with interest, so Tracy and I showed him our gold-plated, seven-tipped-star badges. Al also wanted to see them.

After a moment of silence, Al stated, "See, I told you they were undercover detectives with the sheriff's office."

From that exchange I sensed that Al had a reputation as someone who stretched the truth.

I explained to the pastor that I was thankful that Al had decided to come forward and give us information about the Godfather. I also told him that Al's commitment to helping the community came at a great personal sacrifice. I told him that Al had confessed that the strength to overcome her drug addiction came from her commitment to God.

Al said she knew that the three of us, Tracy, Al, and me, were going to make a great team. Al told her pastor that while I was working undercover with her, she planned to watch my back and that she knew I would watch hers.

Then she looked up to the sky, and said, "He will watch out for both of us. Isn't that right?" She turned and smiled at me.

I replied, "You got that right!"

Before we left, the pastor expressed genuine concern for Al's welfare. He said that in spite of all she had done, she was still God's child.

I thought to myself, *If the Godfather is as big as Al has made him out to be, we will all need someone to watch over us.*

The pastor smiled, then walked back into the church.

Al climbed into the backseat. She said she was glad that we had had a chance to meet her pastor. She told me that if she were paid for her assistance, she would give the money to her church.

That comment prompted me to explain our payment policy to her. I told her that for each drug buy that she helped us with, we would pay her $100. And if her assistance enabled us to execute a search warrant, she would receive a bonus. The amount of the bonus would be based on the number of people arrested, the amount of drugs and money seized, the stolen property recovered, and so on.

She reminded me that she was not helping us for the money. I understood. We agreed that her assistance could not be measured by any monetary standards. No amount of money could repay her for the risks she was taking to bring down the Godfather. I suggested, however, that the money would help her buy some things that she might not otherwise be able to afford. She told me that she did not want to surround herself with material items. She hoped to contribute more to her church. I agreed that that would be a worthwhile way for her to use her money. Many of the informants that we worked with spent their money on drugs and alcohol.

Al suggested that we get down to business. We agreed. She said she had been thinking a lot about how she would help me infiltrate the Godfather's organization. She said she thought that the best way would be for her to introduce me to one of his prostitutes. That was just what I had hoped to avoid. I told Al that we didn't want to get caught up in the prostitution side of his organization. I said with a laugh, "My wife would not like that!"

"As long as I'm with you, none of the girls will lay a hand on you!" Al said.

Al went on to say she thought we should drive to the north side of Indianapolis to meet with Wendy, one of the Godfather's former prostitutes. Wendy had lived with the Godfather and had been one of his best prostitutes; she was now living with a man called Baggy-D.

She said Baggy-D, the son of the director of the Door of Hope Mission, a shelter for homeless men, was one of the Godfather's customers. She warned me that he was crazy and always carried a gun. I asked her if she knew what his real name was. She thought that it was Dante Butters.

I was familiar with the Door of Hope. When I was assigned to the patrol division, we would take men who were down on their luck to the shelter for a meal and a place to sleep. It was a popular place for the homeless during the cold Indiana winters.

I remembered reading an article in the *Indianapolis Register* about the shelter and the outstanding work that the director, Casey Butters, was doing for the community. I wondered if Baggy-D could really be the director's son.

I also wondered why Al would suggest that we needed another person's assistance.

Because of her suggestion, I started to question her ability to help us with the investigation. Was she backing down on some of her claims? What was she leaving out?

Too many times informants lead investigators to believe that they are capable of performing very difficult tasks. Then, as the investigations get underway, they are unable to produce the results they had claimed they could. In this case was Al simply rethinking her strategy or was it the start of a trend of inconsistencies that I would need to monitor?

I explained to Al that if at all possible, I preferred not to have other people involved. I told her that it could get extremely complicated if we used someone who did not realize that he or she was helping an undercover officer in an investigation. There were too many factors that could not be controlled.

"For instance," I said, "What would happen if the person wanted to smoke a marijuana joint in my car while we were driving to the drug dealer's house? Or, what would we tell her if she asked to have some of the drugs that we purchased from the dealer as a payoff for her assistance?"

It would mean that we were supplying this person with drugs, and as officers of the law we couldn't do that.

After she thought about it, Al said she could see my point. But, she explained, it was common for prostitutes to act as go-betweens for the Godfather and his customers. In addition to the money they received for their prostitution services, the Godfather paid them if they were also able to sell drugs to their customers. He frequently profited from selling both prostitution services and drugs to a single customer.

Al said that the Godfather believed that a potential drug customer could not be an undercover officer if he had just slept with a hooker. I saw her point and agreed to meet Wendy if the sergeant would allow to it. I made it very clear, however, that I had no intention of gaining a prostitute's trust by soliciting her services.

Tracy asked Al to describe Wendy and Baggy-D. Tracy did a great job of taking notes. Her notes were always very detailed and easy to follow, which I was glad about because note taking was one of my weaknesses. I couldn't spell very well and my handwriting wasn't good. In every case it's important to write down as much information as possible and not leave out any critical details. So, when I took notes I tried to abbreviate words.

But later I always found it difficult to decipher what I had written. When Tracy took the notes, I was able to concentrate on the information that we needed and the questions I wanted to ask. One of our first questions about Wendy was what she looked like. Because it was critical for Al to know a girl's height, weight, age, race, eye color, hair color, and body measurements when she answered the phone for the Godfather's prostitution service, answering Tracy's question was easy. Al described Wendy as White, thirty-five years old, 5 feet 7 inches, 130 pounds, brown eyes, and long brown hair. Al recited Wendy's measurements: 36C-25-35.

I told Al, "That is the most detailed description that I have ever been given."

She replied, "No problem. That's my job."

Because the prostitutes went by street names, she was not certain what Wendy's real name was. But, Al added, "All you have to do is call Indianapolis vice and they will tell you her name. She might be a good prostitute but she is not very good at avoiding a police sting operation."

According to Al, Wendy once had recognized a vice officer while she was walking the streets. Wendy thought that the vice officer was off-duty and that he wanted some action. But as luck would have it, he wasn't, he didn't, and she went to jail.

Al said that Wendy sometimes would be so strung out on crack cocaine that she would approach a young, good-looking rookie officer and proposition him. She apparently liked men in blue.

I asked myself, *What am I getting into?* I didn't want to have Wendy falling all over me but I had to establish a good rapport with her. If I were lucky, maybe the sergeant would not allow an unwitting person to be involved in the investigation. Sometimes, it was necessary to shift gears in midstream and go with plan B. I had found that in my line of work, I had to be prepared for anything. But if the sergeant did allow it, I would have to gain Wendy's trust without getting into a compromising situation.

Al said that Wendy and Baggy-D lived in a bright yellow ranch-style house on Olson, just north of Boston Avenue. She thought there was a "For Sale" sign in the yard. Wendy had told her that Baggy-D's father owned the house and allowed him to live there rent-free. She described Wendy's relationship with Baggy-D as a business arrangement, not a romantic one.

Tracy asked Al how she would describe Baggy-D. Al said that he looked like a demon, with piercing brown eyes that seemed to look right through a person. She also said that his eyes protruded out of their sockets further than normal, which added to his possessed look.

Al believed that Baggy-D was thirty-six years old, 5 feet 10 inches tall, and 160 pounds. She said that he was White and had long brown hair and a beard. Overall, she said that he was very well-kept and thought of himself as a ladies man. She offered to give me a picture of him. Apparently, he had had his picture taken at a studio and handed them out to his lady friends. I suggested that she could run it out to me when we dropped her off at her house later.

If, as Al indicated, Baggy-D were a heavy user of methamphetamine, or meth, and had a habit of carrying a gun, he would add some danger to the investigation. In general, we were running into more and more people acting very paranoid as a result of using methamphetamine. It was also known as crank, speed, meth, go-fast, and a host of other street names and was relatively new in Indiana. During the early 1990s, it was commonly found among the biker gangs, then it gradually became popular among all types of people. Before then, cocaine was the drug of choice.

With the insurgence of meth, there came stories of people staying up for three or four days at a time. The users also feared that people were after them, including the police. Domestic abuse calls increased. Other common side effects of methamphetamine included severe weight loss, the yellowing and decaying of the teeth, and open sores similar to acne all over the face and body.

The risk of violence in an undercover investigation increased when working with a person like Baggy-D. Even the best communication skills were sometimes not enough to keep a situation from getting out of hand. One of the biggest obstacles to overcome when working undercover was the trust factor. When addicts used methamphetamine, they didn't even trust the people closest to them, let alone a complete stranger. The fact that undercover officers didn't use drugs when they were offered made it even more difficult to gain an addict's confidence.

There were more undercover operations taking place in the Indianapolis area than ever before. Because of that, drug dealers were regularly offering potential new customers samples at their first meetings. Many dealers just refused to sell drugs to someone that they'd just met.

So turning down an offer to try a sample of a drug at the first meeting with a drug dealer could be a clear indication that we were either cops or informants. Knowing that a dealer who uses meth would be even more suspicious added yet another obstacle for an undercover officer to overcome. When dealing with an armed "meth head," safety was severely compromised.

Al said Baggy-D primarily sold methamphetamine. However, he also usually had small amounts of cocaine and crack to sell. She thought that if we asked Baggy-D for a larger amount of crack than he had, he would have to send Wendy to pick it up from the Godfather or take me there to get it. If I were given a choice, I wanted to deal with Wendy as Baggy-D sounded like too big a risk. Also, Al made it sound like the Godfather really trusted Wendy, so I thought he would be more accepting of me if I were with her.

I told Al that Tracy and I had to learn more about Wendy and Baggy-D before we tried to buy drugs from them. By this time we had been talking with Al in the church parking lot for about two hours. It was nearly lunchtime and we were getting hungry. Tracy skimmed her notes and clarified a few items with Al, and then we headed to Al's house.

Along the way, Al asked me how long it might be before we would start our undercover work. I explained that in addition to the necessary background work that we needed to do, I had to sit down with the sergeant and update him on the new information that we had collected and the next steps that we hoped to take in the investigation.

As we pulled into Al's driveway, she spotted her nephew walking down the street toward her house. She said that he was a no-good punk who would frequently steal from her. He appeared to be about twenty-seven years old and 5 feet 7 inches. He was

White, thin, and had long, greasy, brown hair. His clothes were oversized and it looked like he had been wearing them for several days. She cautioned us to be careful about what we said around him. She thought that her nephew would sell her out in exchange for drugs.

I asked Al how her nephew got around town. She said that he walked wherever he went, hitchhiking along the way. If he ran across something worth stealing, he would take it and trade it for drugs. Al opened the car door. She told him that she was busy and that he should come back later. He slowly turned and walked away.

Al hurried into the house. Moments later, she returned with the picture of Baggy-D. Al had described him to a T. He looked like an actor from an Alfred Hitchcock movie. Tracy said she didn't find anything attractive about him. Most of the time drug-addicted women looked past a dealer's appearance and focused on the drugs that he could provide. We thanked Al and told her that we would call her as soon as we were ready to get started.

As we drove back to the office, Tracy said that she, too, was concerned about Al's suggestion that Wendy should be the one who would introduce me to the Godfather. Tracy was aware of the potential for trouble that working with a prostitute could bring.

"You know Wendy is going to expect something for her efforts, and you just might be that something!" she said laughing.

"No thanks," I muttered, shaking my head.

I told Tracy that I thought it was too early to discount Al's usefulness simply because she felt that it would be better to have Wendy introduce me to the Godfather. It would, I admitted, definitely impact the case if Al did not live up to her claims regarding the investigation.

As soon as we got back to the office, the sergeant called Tracy and me into his office for an update on our investigation. I chose my words carefully as I briefed him about our meeting with Al. I wanted to minimize the fact that she had changed her mind about introducing me to the Godfather herself.

Still, he picked up on it and asked me point-blank, "Are you having trouble controlling your informant?"

I explained that her most recent suggestion concerned me, but that I intended to stay on top of the investigation. I would not allow Al to take control of it. I asked him to have confidence in me.

He replied, "If Al is not providing you with accurate information, I will stop the investigation before it leads to someone getting hurt." He then asked me if we had identified Baggy-D or Wendy yet.

I assured him that that would be our next move.

He said that prior to arranging a buy with anyone involved in the Godfather's organization, he wanted to approve the plan, especially since our informant was beginning to show signs of inconsistency. "Is that understood?" he asked.

"Yes, sir. It is," I said.

We left his office; we had work to do. As we walked down the hallway toward my office, I looked at Tracy and shrugged. Why did he ask us if we had identified Baggy-D and Wendy yet? Of course, we hadn't. We couldn't have identified them between the time we left Al's house and the time we arrived back at the office. It must have been his way of telling us what to do next.

# Chapter 5

That afternoon, Tracy and I took a break from our case to help Stuart with an undercover buy of methamphetamine. An informant had told Stuart that she had spoken with the dealer the night before. She had made arrangements to buy an eighth of an ounce of meth from him. The meth dealer told her to come over anytime the next day, and he would have it ready for her.

David, Stuart, Tracy, Joe, and I met the informant in a shopping center parking lot. Stuart asked Tracy to frisk the informant. The informant was a petite Hispanic female, twenty-three years old, and neatly dressed. It was common practice for us to frisk informants to ensure that they did not have any drugs on them prior to attempting a buy. It was the only way we could be sure when informants returned with drugs after meeting with dealers that the drugs had been given to them by the dealers in their homes or places of business. It prevented informants from compromising investigations.

Occasionally an informant would have a change of heart and would try to discredit an investigation. For example, sometimes they said that the drugs didn't come from the places for which we had obtained search warrants. They would claim that they had the drugs with them prior to entering the dealers' homes or businesses.

For the same reason, I searched the informant's car. Inevitability, informants showed up with cars that were filled with dirty clothes, baby toys, tools, and other junk, even drugs.

On one occasion, an informant showed up with approximately one ounce of methamphetamine. When the plastic bag of drugs was discovered, he said that his girlfriend had just kicked him out of her apartment and he had no other place to keep his drugs. Stuart had reminded him that he had signed an agreement not to use or possess any illegal substances while working as an informant. The meth was seized as evidence and turned in to the property room. He was notified that he would receive a felony charge in addition to the charges that were already pending against him and he could no longer serve as an informant.

He was found dead a week later of an apparent drug overdose.

Tracy and I concluded our searches without finding any illegal substances or drug paraphernalia, such as smoking pipes or snort tubes with residue inside. I did, however, ask the woman to clean her car out before our next meeting. She glared at me, saying that that was how her car always looked and it would be out of character for her to show up at someone's house with a clean car. It might raise some suspicion. I asked her if she would consider a compromise and remove half of the items.

"Whatever," she said dismissively.

Reminding myself that while working with informants is one of a detective's most difficult tasks, it's also one of the most critical parts of an investigation, I ignored her attitude.

Stuart handed the informant money and a bug, a concealed electronic listening device. He instructed her to drive directly to the dealer's house. Upon the conclusion of the drug buy, she was to return to the shopping center parking lot.

She said that she understood and jumped into her car. The first thing that she did was turn up the volume on her car stereo. The type of music that she was listening to was not what I would have chosen, but it made it obvious that the bug was working. The signal was strong and it sounded as though I was sitting right next to her. She was about fifteen years younger than me and it showed in her taste of music. The song's pounding bass could be heard throughout the parking lot. I was glad that we only had to follow her a few miles and not across town.

It must have been her way of trying to relax and get into the proper mind-set for her first buy as an informant. Not only do undercover officers need to be mentally prepared, but so do informants. Even though they have purchased drugs from the dealers many times before, the first time that they are required to turn the drugs over to another person without profiting from their efforts – either by consuming some of the drugs or by selling the drugs to others – feels strange.

Some informants enjoy the "high" that they experience when buying drugs as part of an undercover operation. They say that while the risk of getting caught by the police is eliminated, it is replaced by the thrill of wearing a bug and by the challenge of keeping secret their identity as an informant.

Stuart motioned for the informant to take off. She left the parking lot as if the official starter to a race had dropped the green flag. She was not only exceeding the speed limit but she was also weaving in and out of traffic. The sergeant radioed to Stuart and instructed him to have her slow down. We didn't want to have an accident while trying to follow the informant to the drug dealer's house. Stuart was able to pull up beside her car as she stopped for a red light and let her know she was going too fast.

When we arrived at the suspected drug dealer's apartment complex, I followed the informant inside the building. We were required to follow an informant inside and actually watch her enter the suspected drug dealer's apartment. The informant did not know that a detective would be following her inside. It was one way for us to test the informant's integrity. I stopped at the mailboxes, which were on the first floor, just inside the front door. She walked down the hallway toward apartment No. 5. I pretended to scan the names on the mailboxes.

Out of the corner of my eye, I saw her stop and knock on the door of No. 5. She did not seem to be looking around, so I was almost certain that she did not know that she was being followed.

Moments later, the door to the apartment opened and she stepped inside. After hearing the door close, I turned and left the apartment building. I got back in the car. Tracy had remained in the car and was monitoring the conversation between the informant and the drug dealer. Tracy said that the informant was doing a good job and didn't seem to be nervous.

I asked Tracy to let me know if the informant was getting ready to leave the apartment. I needed to go back inside the building and watch the informant leave the apartment in order to verify that the drugs were purchased from someone inside apartment No. 5.

On Tracy's signal, I reentered the building, making every effort to blend into the neighborhood. I saw the informant come out of apartment No. 5, walk down the hallway, and exit the building. I followed her out and got back in the car.

We all met back at the shopping center parking lot. When I arrived, the informant was being debriefed. Apparently the buy had been successful. The informant was not only able to purchase the desired quantity of drugs, but she also saw a large amount of methamphetamine, a scale, and a box of plastic bags sitting on a glass end table.

# Chapter 6

The next day, we had our biweekly intelligence meeting, which involved detectives from several area law enforcement agencies. When it was my turn, I asked for any information that the various agencies might have about the Godfather. Several in attendance were criminal analysts from the Indiana National Guard. They were assigned to the federal government's Counter Drug Task Force. They agreed to check their intelligence database for information on the Godfather.

Several days passed before a task force member with the Drug Enforcement Administration (DEA) let me know he'd found a report that he had written following an April 1990 interview with an Orange County Jail inmate. According to the report, the inmate, who was facing state drug charges, had stated that the Godfather, a man in his fifties, was a "cooker" of methamphetamine. The inmate said he had lived on the Godfather's property at 1000 S.E. Lexington, Indianapolis, at various times over the past few years.

According to the inmate, the Godfather regularly cooked up a quarter pound of methamphetamine and stored it in plastic bags. The inmate also told the DEA agent that the Godfather had been in the narcotics trafficking business in Indianapolis since 1988 or 1989, that he carried weapons, and that he always had large sums of money at his house.

The inmate had added that the Godfather was careful not to show any outward signs of wealth or drive flashy cars to avoid attracting attention from law enforcement.

I also learned that the Federal Bureau of Investigations (FBI) had collected information in December 1991 that confirmed that the Godfather possessed numerous weapons and kept them on his property.

A report from the Indianapolis Police Department mentioned two crime alert calls in 1992 from an anonymous caller who said that a White man living at 1000 S.E. Lexington, Indianapolis, was selling illegal drugs. The anonymous caller stated that this same man was operating an out-call prostitution service and had a lot of weapons stored on his property.

In addition, Special Agent Tom Bowersox of the United States Secret Service called me to say that he had conducted an interview with a female inmate at the Lasage County Sheriff's Office in Knoxville, Indiana, in November 1994. During the interview, the inmate from Indianapolis, provided information about a big drug dealer in the area. She said the dealer could supply any amount of cocaine or methamphetamine that a person wanted to buy. The inmate, who had been arrested for fraud, stated that during the first or second week of February 1994, she was at a house in the Bottoms on the southeast side of Indianapolis. There she witnessed a large quantity of illegal drugs being sold by a man she knew as the Godfather. She told Special Agent Bowersox that her boyfriend frequently purchased drugs from the Godfather.

She said that the Godfather's real name was Robert Fisher and that he was a White man, approximately 5 feet 9 inches tall, with brownish-gray hair. She described the Godfather's house as being north of Moulton by the railroad tracks, which was the same general location as 1000 S.E. Lexington, and provided his phone number.

She also told the agent that the Godfather was a prime source for guns in the Indianapolis area. She claimed that a man named Kirby Homes, a regular drug customer of the Godfather's, had weapons in his possession during a February 1994 raid that had been given to Homes by the Godfather.

I did a background check on Kirby Homes and discovered that he had a prior drug arrest. In February 1994, he had been arrested by the Indianapolis Police Department and charged with the possession of a controlled substance with the intent to deliver and the possession of a weapon carried by a felon.

I also spoke with a Lasage County Deputy about a statement that he had taken from a female inmate in the Lasage County Jail. The deputy said that she had told him that Marcus and Dwayne Morrill were at the Godfather's house on a regular basis and were customers of the Godfather's.

By themselves, the individual bits of information I received from the various agencies were not enough to obtain a search warrant or make an arrest. But when combined with the information that I collected, they were of great value. I felt as though a picture of the Godfather was becoming clearer.

I was more sure than ever that it takes a team effort by the various law enforcement agencies to bring down a top-level criminal or organization. I had to hope, however, that the interviewing and writing skills of the other investigators were solid.

Interviewing a person was one of the more interesting aspects of my job. But along with it came the task of putting the information down on paper. In other words, I had to write reports.

On television, police dramas spend very little time showing the detectives at their desks typing their reports or, like I did, dictating them. If they would show how much time is actually spent completing investigation reports, viewers would be bored and would not watch the programs. Crime dramas are watched for their action and suspense. But in real life, investigations are not always filled with continuous action.

During an investigation, we had to record the facts that pertained to each and every event as they unfolded. Later, we would sit down and expand on our reports by clarifying the chain of events and filling in the details.

During most of our investigations, a detective was assigned to do nothing more than record times and write short narratives of the events that were taking place.

While writing reports was not exciting and was very time-consuming, it was the reports that created the foundation of a solid case. If an interview was three to four hours long, it generally took at least the same amount of time to write the report. A good investigator knew better than to rely solely on his memory. He needed thorough reports. Many times, the details provided critical evidence when convicting a person or group of conspirators.

While I was in the middle of organizing all this new information, the sergeant asked for an update on the Godfather. I told him about the information I had received from the various local and federal agencies. He asked if we had confirmed any of the information. I said that we had verified some of it, but that much of it had been obtained through anonymous calls.

"There appears to be sufficient cause to spend more time on this investigation," he said. "I want you to put your other cases on the back burner and concentrate on this one."

However, he said he would not ask any of the other members of our unit to help us. Besides not getting the assistance I thought a case of this magnitude deserved, it meant that Tracy and I would be expected to assist the other detectives with their cases.

So, we proceeded on our own. I called Al and asked her if she had heard anything from Baggy-D or Wendy. Al said that she had talked with them and that they were willing to meet with us.

"However, you better get your butts in gear," she said. "I've been waiting to hear from you guys. What's the holdup? You can't expect me to line up a deal for you and then not hear anything from you for a couple of days!"

I tried to explain that she needed to check with me before setting anything up because there were policies I had to follow and other cases to work. I told her I could not cut corners and put a deal together simply at her request.

It seemed to go in one ear and out the other; she did not want to hear about the unit's policies. I couldn't say that I blamed her. Sometimes there seemed to be a lot of red tape to cut through in order to get anything accomplished.

I told Al that I needed to verify the identities of Wendy and Baggy-D, but that we might be able to set up our first drug buy the next day. In the meantime, I asked her not to say anything about me when she spoke with them. I wanted to work on my undercover identity. As I finished my explanation, I could hear excitement in her voice.

That night, I talked with Paula about the investigation. I told her that because of the complexity of the Godfather's organization, I thought I needed to take over as Al's primary contact. I originally had told Tracy that Al would be her informant. But now, with so much at stake, I didn't think that was wise. Tracy was a very good rookie detective, but I didn't feel she was experienced enough to take on the responsibility of such an important investigation. This would give Tracy the opportunity to be second in charge of an investigation and to learn from me as we worked on the case together. I told Paula that I hoped that Tracy would understand and not feel bad. In the back of my mind I wondered if I was being selfish. I knew the case could turn out to be the "big one" I'd been waiting for.

Paula said that I should explain to Tracy that my decision was meant to alleviate the pressure that the sergeant might put on her and that I was not cutting her out of the case. I told Paula that I felt that Tracy was mature and could handle the shift in responsibilities.

"You sure do think a lot of Tracy, don't you!" Paula said.

"Yes, I do. She is learning quickly and is a big asset to the unit," I said. "Tracy is the first woman that has been assigned to our unit and she brings a new dimension."

What was Paula implying? Was she concerned that I was spending too much time with a female co-worker? Paula's comment made me feel uncomfortable. "What do you mean?" I asked.

Paula said that she had never heard me make so many positive comments about another woman and that it bothered her that I talked about Tracy's abilities, how well she was doing, and how well we worked together.

I stopped and thought for a minute. I had been talking a lot about Tracy. But I was simply sharing the day's events with my wife.

Paula continued, "If the roles were reversed and I was working daily with a man, how would that make you feel? If I came home at night and routinely made conversation about him, wouldn't that upset you?"

"Of course I would feel uncomfortable with it," I said, suddenly realizing that I might have a double standard in this instance.

At times, Paula's outgoing personality made me uncomfortable. This was the second marriage for both of us. I had a lot of unresolved issues left over from my first marriage, which meant that I had to work that much harder at making my second marriage work.

I had been married to my first wife, Carla, for thirteen years. Carla was like me, more reserved and comfortable not being the center of attention in social settings. In thirteen years, I never once was jealous of Carla.

On the other hand, Paula was full of confidence and energy. People were attracted to her because of her outgoing personality. When we were out with friends or family, she was always at the center of things.

As a result of our different personality types, Paula and I frequently challenged each other as we tried to establish our roles within our marriage. This created a lot of friction between us. The same personality traits that had attracted us to each other were a source of conflict.

Paula was experiencing her own adjustments, the biggest of which was moving with her children from Illinois to Indiana so that I could continue my career. She missed her family and friends.

Paula said emphatically, "I know how a woman thinks. You don't always see things from the perspective I do. Tracy is no different than any other woman just because she is a police officer!"

"I don't think Tracy desires anything more that a professional relationship," I said.

Paula switched gears, reminding me about the time I had had an informant taken away from me in a similar type of case. She said, "Just remember the way you felt in the Kimm conspiracy. I'm sure you can try to make Tracy feel better about her new role than the way you were made to feel."

I did not want Tracy to feel as I had. I told Paula that I would do everything in my power to keep Tracy involved in the investigation of the Godfather. My only hope was that the case might be even half as productive as the Kimm investigation, which had resulted in the indictment and conviction of twenty-seven members of the Kimm organization.

# Chapter 7

Paula seemed to be preoccupied the next morning. She was quieter than usual. Did I dare ask if Tracy was still on her mind? She walked into the boys' bedroom and woke them up. Paula gave me a dirty look as she walked down the hall. I wasn't sure what I'd done, but there was no time to ask as Paula had a 7 a.m. meeting at work and was out the door.

As I was getting something for the boys to eat, my mind was wandering. I was thinking about my plans for the day when I heard Joel say, "It was an accident."

I looked over and saw that he had spilled milk on the table. The sound of his voice was a reminder to me that I still had things to do at home before I could even think about work.

Joel smiled at me. When Joel smiled at me, any feelings that I had of being upset were quickly forgotten.

I smiled back. "Try to be more careful the next time," I said, grabbing a paper towel and wiping off the table. Nate and Joel went back to watching cartoons and eating their breakfast. Again, I found myself thinking about my workday.

After finding Nate's shoes and book bag, we were out the door. The boys fastened their seat belts and we were off to day care. It was comforting to know that Paula was the assistant director at their day-care center.

It allowed them to see her periodically throughout the day. Paula would often drive Nate to school in the day-care van with the other children. Paula was also able to visit Joel's classroom from time to time.

As we entered the building, Paula was busy talking with one of the parents. Joel raced up to her and gave her a hug. She smiled at Nate and at me. When Nate walked past her, Paula said, "Where's my hug?" He was embarrassed. He gave her a quick hug and left to find his friends.

Joel gave me a big hug and said, "Good-bye." He turned and walked towards his classroom. I had been around Joel since he was two and a half years old. We had a comfortable relationship, more comfortable than the one that I had with Nate.

Nate was three years older than Joel. He was old enough to understand that he was no longer living with his father. Seeing his father only every two weeks was difficult for him, especially since they lived in different states. It weighed heavily on Paula's mind.

Paula asked how I was doing. I admitted that I was anxious to get to work and talk with the sergeant about Tracy and Al. We talked a few more minutes, than I headed off to work.

While driving to the office, I tried to think of the best way to approach the sergeant. My past experiences with him had taught me that I had to let him make the decisions.

I walked into his office and found him reading the morning paper. It was part of his routine and it fed his memory, which was amazing. Reading a story in the paper could prompt him to remember a person or event that had occurred years before. His ability to remember facts about people made him a valuable resource for the department.

I really hadn't decided how I was going to approach him with my dilemma. I tried to pick my words carefully. I wanted to appear confident, but not cocky. He interrupted me and said, "Don't sugarcoat it. What do you want?"

I told him that I needed his advice on how I could work on the case, and at the same time, give Tracy experience on how to manage an informant. I admitted that I had originally told Tracy that she would be Al's primary contact. At this point, when Al needed something or she wanted to make contact with us, Al called Tracy. It was also Tracy's responsibility to call Al daily to ensure that she was not getting sidetracked or slipping away from her mission.

I explained to the sergeant that I was questioning if Tracy was ready to take on the challenge of managing an informant. If our preliminary investigation was accurate, I wanted to be the one responsible for managing Al's involvement.

The sergeant asked me if I thought that Tracy was capable of handling Al and all of the responsibilities associated with dealing with an informant.

He wondered if she could control Al's activities and prevent Al from returning to her crack addiction, and if she possessed the insight on how to build a case that would lead to the arrest and conviction of the Godfather and bring down his organization.

I needed to address each of the sergeant's questions, but I felt as though I needed to tap dance a little. I didn't want to minimize Tracy's abilities. But at the same time, in my opinion, she simply wasn't ready to take on the responsibility of handling the informant in such an important case. We all make mistakes. However, if Tracy made any mistakes with Al, it could cost us the investigation. An officer's safety might even be compromised. I didn't want to take that chance.

In addition, I was concerned about how the sergeant would critique my performance as her training officer. Would he think that I was moving too slowly with her training and not teaching her properly? I wasn't experienced in training undercover officers. I was still learning how to handle the job myself. Even though I didn't consider myself a rookie any longer, I was a long way from feeling like an expert.

I thought a minute, then simply advised him that Tracy had a good rapport with Al. I said I thought she would attempt to keep Al away from drugs by maintaining as much contact with Al as possible. She would also be available to provide support when Al needed it.

After several more minutes of questions and answers, the sergeant made his decision. "Use your own judgment," he said.

I had gotten lucky. He had left the door open. I could begin my discussion with Tracy by stating, "Following a meeting with the sergeant, ..."

The morning meeting was scheduled to start in twenty minutes, which gave me some time to plan my day. I would start my day by talking with Tracy about the Godfather investigation.

Together we would plan our next move. I also needed to set aside time to dictate the information that I had learned about the Godfather the day before. Tracy, I had noticed, procrastinated when it came to dictating her reports. I needed to remind her that it was important to set aside time each day in order to keep her reports current. This was a natural adjustment for officers new to the unit as patrol officers wrote or typed their reports. Dictation was unfamiliar to them.

For me, learning to dictate was not easy. I found a written report easier to follow, and expressing my thoughts out loud in a narrative manner was not natural. It took time and practice before I had gotten better at it. For a while, at the suggestion of my training officer, I wrote my reports first, then read them into a recorder. I found the two-step process too time-consuming, however, and went back to just dictating.

Frequently, I found myself stopping the recorder and rewinding the tape to listen to what I had already dictated because it was hard to remember whether or not I had mentioned a particular fact or series of events.

When Stephanie, our secretary, returned the first few dictated reports that I had not written out first, I discovered that I had a lot of work to do. I had repeated myself on the one hand and, on the other, had left out important details all together. Some of my sentences were difficult to follow.

At that point I had decided that I needed to concentrate on mastering dictation as many people formed their first impressions of undercover officers by reading our reports. In many situations, a person's only contact with us might be through our reports. Many people in the criminal justice system had access to the reports, including the intake attorneys who approved the filing of criminal charges, the prosecuting attorneys, the defense attorneys and their investigators, and the probation and parole officers.

It took a lot of effort on my part but, eventually, I became comfortable with my ability to dictate reports.

Remembering how difficult it was to make the transition from writing to dictating reports, I could understand what Tracy might be going through. But I didn't want her to fall into a pattern of procrastination. Some officers put off writing their reports as long as they could, then condensed the information in their reports in order to get them done. In doing so, they omitted many important details. It was easy for good defense attorneys to find holes in those types of reports and use those holes to plant seeds of doubt in the minds of jurors and judges.

I decided I was going to do my best to help Tracy become proficient at dictating her reports.

My thoughts were interrupted by the sergeant announcing over the intercom, "Meeting, five minutes."

Tracy walked into my office and sat down. "What's our day look like today?" she asked.

Tracy looked as if she had gotten very little sleep. Her eyes were puffy and not as clear as they normally were. I asked her, "Was it a rough night?"

"Yes, Jason and I were up talking until 1 a.m. What an ass!" she exclaimed. "I'll tell you about it later."

Jason was going to be her ex-husband soon. They had been married about ten years. Unfortunately, their marriage was ending on bad terms. Tracy had a fourteen year-old daughter from a previous marriage and, according to Tracy, Jason was like a father to her daughter.

Tracy was about my age and very attractive. But the divorce was taking its toll on her. She had lost a lot of weight and was not sleeping well.

Some people felt better at work, away from their problems, while others were so upset by the events taking place in their lives that their work suffered. Tracy appeared to stay focused at work. But occasionally, she had a bad day. If today had already gotten off to a bad start for her, I realized I would have to be especially sensitive when I talked with her about Al.

"I'm sorry. It sounds like you had a rough night," I said. "Want to talk about it?"

She tried to smile, but was obviously upset. She put on her game face and walked out of my office. The unit meeting was about to begin.

Stuart went first. He told us that the day before, David and he had met with a woman at patrol headquarters. The woman had been stopped by one of the road deputies and was in possession of a small amount of methamphetamine.

The woman said that instead of facing possible jail time or a fine, she wanted to cooperate, which meant that she would be required to participate in three new drug investigations. The cases had to lead to the execution of a search warrant for a drug house or the introduction of an undercover officer to a person who was selling drugs.

Stuart told us the name of the woman that they had interviewed and that she was able to make drug buys at five different houses. The sergeant interrupted Stuart and asked him how important the drug dealers were.

"I didn't recognize the names or addresses of any of the people she gave us. But she said she can buy several grams from each of them," Stuart answered.

"Just make sure we're not wasting money on small-time targets! Things are getting busy around here, and we don't have the time to waste running around buying gram amounts of dope!" the sergeant said.

After a brief moment of silence, Stuart continued to discuss the various facts about the people she could buy from.

When Stuart was done, we each took turns informing the unit about the information that we had gathered the previous day.

As I listened to the other members of the unit give their reports, it became clear to me that we would not have to help with any other investigations that day. With that in mind, I could plan my day accordingly. I had a lot of work to do in order to put together a drug buy from Baggy-D and Wendy.

The sergeant ended the meeting by saying, "Get your informants up and working! I want to buy dope today."

Tracy walked into her office, which was within earshot of my office. She closed the door. She did not want to be interrupted. I knew that she was taking time out to take care of some personal things, or "government work," as we called it.

She was probably going to call Jason. If so, she might be on the phone for only twenty seconds or for as long as twenty minutes. I just hoped that the sergeant would not walk by and notice that Tracy's door was closed. If he did, he would knock and go inside to see what she was doing.

I was anxious to learn more about Baggy-D and Wendy, so I opened the case file on the Godfather. I was hoping to find the information that Al had given us about Baggy-D and Wendy.

The thickness of the case jacket reflected the amount of time that we had already devoted to the investigation. After thumbing through several reports, I came across the one I wanted.

The report said Al had stated that she thought Baggy-D's name was actually Dante Butters and that she had heard that Baggy-D's father was involved with the Door of Hope Mission. That was where I would start.

I looked up the listing for the Door of Hope Mission in the phone book and dialed it.

"Door of Hope Mission, how may I help you?" said the man who answered the phone.

"Yes, I was hoping you might be able to help me," I said. "Can you tell me who the director currently is?"

"Yes, that would be Mr. Butters," he said. "Would you like to speak with him?"

"No, that's okay. I'm trying to locate his son. I haven't seen him for some time," I said. "The last I knew, his dad was working at the Door of Hope, and I thought that he might be able to tell me how to get in touch with his son."

"I'm sure he can. Which son is that, Andrew or Dante?" he asked.

"I'm sorry. Dante," I said. "We were classmates and our reunion is coming up."

"I know what a task that must be, trying to find current addresses for everybody," he said. "Mr. Butters is not in at the moment. If you would give me your name and phone number, Mr. Butters can call you back when he returns."

"Thank-you very much, but I'm just leaving the office and I'm not sure when I'll be returning," I replied. "I will try to call Mr. Butters some other time."

"Okay. Well, have a nice day and good luck with your reunion," the man concluded politely.

I thanked him again for his time and hung up. I had just verified the information about Baggy-D that Al had given us. Unless there was more than one Dante Butters, his father was the director of the Door of Hope Mission.

Sometimes I felt uncomfortable misrepresenting myself like that. I had lied to a very helpful man. But nevertheless, when working undercover, it was an acceptable method used to obtain information for an investigation.

I could hear Tracy's door open. It sounded like she was walking away from her office. Maybe this would be a good time for us to discuss the changes that I wanted to make. But on the other hand, the timing probably wasn't the best, especially if she had just gotten off the phone with Jason.

When she returned to her office, I asked, "Tracy, do you have a moment?"

I could see that her eyes were red and swollen; she had a wadded-up tissue in her hand.

"Are you okay?" I asked.

"Just another day of hell," she replied.

"Let's go for a ride," I suggested.

"I could use a Pepsi," she said, fighting hard to hold back tears. "I'll meet you at your car in five minutes."

I reviewed Al's description of where Baggy-D and Wendy lived, and then stepped into Stephanie's office. "Tracy and I are going to drive to the Highland Park area of Indianapolis to attempt to locate an address," I told her.

Stephanie had been working in the drug unit for several years, and we'd become good friends over that time.

"Tracy is outside waiting for you," Stephanie said.

When I got outside I found Tracy sitting in the passenger's seat of my car. She had her window down and was smoking a cigarette. Both were signs of Tracy's stress as she generally drove when we went somewhere and she knew I didn't appreciate her smoking, as I didn't smoke. In fact, Paula got mad when my clothes carried the smell of smoke into the house.

"Why don't you ask Tracy not to smoke in your car?" Paula always demanded when I got home and smelled of smoke.

It put me in a tough spot. While I didn't like to be in such close proximity to someone who was smoking, I didn't want to offend Tracy by asking her not to smoke when we were together. I ignored it this time, too, and drove to a convenience store so that Tracy could buy a Pepsi.

"Do you want anything?" Tracy asked as she stepped out of the car.

"No thanks. I'm fine," I replied.

When she got back into the car, she had her can of pop and was eating a breakfast sandwich.

"I'm ready now. Where are we going?" she asked.

"I thought you might want to get out of the office for a while, so I thought we could attempt to find where Baggy-D and Wendy live," I suggested.

"Cool, let's go," Tracy said.

She was sounding better already. I hoped that her burst of energy would help to put her in a better frame of mind so that we could talk about the case. But first I thought we should cover the personal stuff. I considered her a good friend and wanted to help if I could.

"Do you want to talk about your phone call to Jason?" I asked.

"There isn't much to say really. It's the same old bullshit," she replied. "But thanks for asking. I'll just have to work through his latest demands in the divorce by myself. I called my attorney and told him what Jason is trying to pull with our land."

Tracy and Jason owned some property outside of Indianapolis. They farmed it in addition to working for the sheriff's office. Tracy said that she had worked just as hard on the farm as Jason did and that she wanted what she was entitled to as far as the property was concerned.

As we headed toward Baggy-D's house, I decided to talk with Tracy about my meeting with the sergeant.

"The sergeant and I spoke about your training this morning," I told her. "Because of the stress you're experiencing with your divorce, I want to help lighten the load if I can. Please don't take what I'm about to say as a reflection of your ability."

Tracy looked puzzled. "Okay," she said slowly.

"For the time being, I think it would be best if I were the primary contact for Al," I said. "You will continue to have equal input into the investigation. This will simply mean that if the sergeant is unhappy with something we are doing, he will jump on me and not you."

"So, Al will be your informant from now on?" Tracy asked.

"Was this the sergeant's call or yours?"

"Mine, I guess. He left the decision up to me," I replied. "But, I don't view her as my informant. I'll simply take more of an active role when Al contacts us and provides information."

Tracy sat quietly for a while. I wondered what was going through her mind. Did she feel as if I was stealing her informant? I hoped that she wasn't questioning her abilities as a rookie investigator. Then, Tracy attempted a smile and whispered, "Okay."

Because of the many adjustments that she had to make in her personal life, maybe she would consider the change in the investigation as minor and it wouldn't be a big deal to her. At least she wasn't being cut completely out of the case as had happened to me once.

I just hoped that my ability to handle Al would result in a stronger case against the Godfather.

# Chapter 8

I described to Tracy my phone call to the Door of Hope Mission. I wanted her to have the latest information and an example of one way an undercover officer can operate.

When I was a rookie, I found that watching and listening to the more experienced detectives made my transition into undercover roles easier. Being exposed to their undercover expertise also helped me to expand my own creativity and imagination. I was better prepared to gather information.

"Let's go," Tracy said. "If we learn more about Baggy-D, maybe the sergeant will let us try to make a buy from him. Didn't Al tell us his house was a yellow ranch and was in the area of Olson and Boston? I think Al also said there was a 'For Sale' sign in his front yard. Maybe that will help us as well."

As we got closer to the area where Al said Baggy-D and Wendy lived, I slowed down. "What will we want to do on our initial observation of the house?" I asked Tracy.

"If we plan to do an undercover buy, it would probably be better if we didn't actually drive past the house. Right?" she asked.

"You're right," I replied. "What other option do we have?"

"Keeping in mind that we are not in our surveillance van, we don't want to get very close," she said. "If we can locate the house from a distance, we can return later in the van. Then we can park close enough to the residence to record the house number, vehicle descriptions, and license plate numbers on the vehicles parked near the house."

"Look, there is a small yellow ranch house."

I caught a glimpse of a yellow house as we passed the 2500 block of Boston. It was about four to five houses north of the intersection of Boston and Olson, the exact location Al had described.

We hurried back to the office. I asked Tracy to get the camera and put it in the surveillance van. Then I told Stephanie that Tracy and I were going to take the van out for about thirty minutes.

"Al called for Tracy," Stephanie reported.

I explained to Stephanie that I was now Al's contact.

"Have you informed Al about the change yet?" Stephanie asked.

"No, I haven't. I'll call her after we confirm the address on the house," I replied.

Tracy and I stuck a couple of magnetic business signs for A-1 Painting on the sides of the panel van and we were off. The signs allowed us to blend into the neighborhood without raising any suspicions.

The van, once a stolen vehicle recovered by the department, was now a sophisticated and fully equipped surveillance vehicle.

Tracy and I drove past the yellow house that we thought belonged to Baggy-D and Wendy. The address posted on the house was 2605 Olson. Tracy drove a little further down the street and parked.

We carefully studied the small, ranch-style house. The property was well kept and sat among other middle-class homes. It had a gravel driveway and a "For Sale" sign was posted in the front yard. There were no cars that we could associate with the house.

We sat there for about thirty minutes. During that time, there was no movement around the house. Either no one was home or the occupants were still sleeping.

"Let's go back to the office," I said to Tracy. It had been a brief surveillance. We hadn't learned much, but it was a start.

On the way back to the office, I asked Tracy what she thought we should do next. She suggested calling the power company now that we had Baggy-D's address. She would attempt to find out who was registered for service at the house, what the length of service was, whether a roommate was listed, the Social Security number of the person registered, and what was listed as his or her place of employment.

As she parked the van, I told Tracy that I would call Al. I went to Stephanie's office to let her know that we were back and to check for any messages. Stephanie said that Al had called again and had sounded excited. She wanted one of us to call her back right away.

I dialed Al's phone number. The phone rang only once before Al answered. As Stephanie had said, Al was enthusiastic.

"I spoke with Baggy-D and Wendy this morning and they want to meet you," she said quickly. "I told them we would be over later today."

Al had forgotten that she was supposed to talk with us before making any commitments to Baggy-D. She continued. Apparently Baggy-D and Wendy had stopped by Al's house unexpectedly. They were both flying high and Baggy-D was flashing a plastic bag filled with a white powdered substance. He'd also given her his new phone number.

Al said she told them that she had a friend from southern Indiana, a wealthy farmer who sold cocaine to local residents, who was looking to get set up with a new dealer.

She told Baggy-D that my sources in southern Indiana were drying up and that he could make a lot of money selling to me. When Al told him that I had money, she said his eyes lit up and he asked when I was going to be in Indianapolis next.

I told Al that it was good news, but we still had things to learn about Baggy-D and Wendy before I could meet with them. I also informed Al that her decision to make up a cover story for me was wrong. I needed to have complete control of my cover.

Next I explained to her that she should not commit to a specific time as to when I would be available to purchase drugs. It could back us into a corner and might make a bad first impression. I asked her to be more vague about her knowledge of my work schedule and the times that I might be available to drive to Indianapolis.

Basically, I asked Al to slow down. I was excited about the possibility of meeting with them, but it was important for me to be the one calling the shots, not Al. Allowing an informant to run a case was a rookie mistake.

I asked Al to contact me instead of Tracy from now on, explaining that because things were heating up and we were getting close to setting up an undercover drug buy, it would be better for me to be her contact.

Because Tracy and Al had already developed a good working relationship and I wanted to keep Tracy involved, I told Al this change was being made to eliminate any chance of something being missed when Al passed along information.

I gave Al my pager number and instructed her to page me anytime and that if possible, I would call her back within ten minutes.

I asked Al if she had seen what kind of car they were driving. She said that she hadn't seen them pull up, and when they left, she had run to the phone to call Tracy and didn't think to look out the window.

I told Al not to call them back until I gave her the go-ahead. If they called her or stopped by again, I instructed her to tell them that she was having problems getting in touch with me. That would give us more time to complete the research that we needed to get done. Al agreed.

Tracy came into my office just as I was finishing my conversation with Al. I asked Al if I could put her on hold for a minute, then quickly explained to Tracy what I had just told Al.

"Can you think of anything else?" I asked Tracy.

"Tell her to keep her lights off at night so that Baggy-D doesn't stop by unexpectedly," she said. "And tell her hello!"

After hanging up, I asked Tracy what she had learned from the power company. "The person who has power at 2605 Olson is Casey Butters. His address is RR 3, Montezuma, Indiana," she said, "However, Dante Craig Butters is living in the house."

The security aid for the power company had also told her that Dante Butter's date of birth was March 11, 1959, his Social Security number was 374-05-8247, and the phone number at the house was 317-555-7053.

"That's the same phone number that Al just gave me," I said.

Tracy volunteered to use the information to check transportation records and run a criminal history check on Baggy-D.

"While you're doing that, I will call the Indianapolis Police Department and speak with someone in vice. Maybe if Wendy is as popular with the police as Al says she is, we can find out who she is," I said.

I looked through the debriefing report and found Al's description of Wendy, then called the police department vice unit.

The secretary that answered said she had not heard of Wendy. She put me on hold to check with an officer.

Someone picked up the line. "So, what do you want to know about Wendy?" a man asked, laughing.

I explained who I was and that I suspected that Wendy might be involved in a drug investigation I was working. I gave the vice officer the description I had of Wendy and asked if it matched one of their regulars.

"It sure does. Wait a minute while I punch her up in the computer," he said.

A short time later, the vice officer returned to the phone.

"We have her name as Wendy Renee Boyd, born September 27, 1960. Her Social Security number is 885-93-4838, and her last known address was 3622 5th Avenue, Indianapolis," he said.

He also said she had been arrested several times for prostitution, interference, and resisting arrest, but never on drug charges. The vice officer told me that he had a picture of her if I wanted to see it. "She's a cute one," he said.

I thanked him for his information and hung up.

Tracy came to my office and we exchanged information. She had found out that Baggy-D had been arrested four times since 1978 for driving while intoxicated, domestic abuse, and possession of marijuana. He had also had several minor convictions in the state of Florida, one a marijuana charge. In addition, one of his drunk driving charges had come from our department.

After telling Tracy about Wendy, I suggested we drive down to the county jail to pick up a picture of Wendy. And since we were there, we might as well pickup Baggy-D's picture.

"After we pick up the pictures, we can put together a game plan," I said. "Then we'll ask the sergeant for permission to make a buy from them."

The jail clerk had to look in the basement for the files. After twenty minutes of searching, she returned with two pictures. We photocopied them and went back to the office.

Tracy and I were both excited about the information we had uncovered. So far, all of Al's information had checked out. She was gaining credibility.

When working with a new informant, it was important to have a certain amount of trust in him or her. Ironically, we would be going into a drug dealer's house based upon the trust that the drug dealer had in the informant. We had to be certain that no matter what happened, the informant would assist us in getting out safely.

Back at the office, we discussed various scenarios that would give Al the opportunity to introduce me to Baggy-D and Wendy. After a while, I suggested that Tracy call Al to see if she was available to meet with us.

"What time should I tell her we will pick her up?" she asked.

"Forty-five minutes. And, ask her to come out to our car," I said.

While Tracy called Al, I went into Stephanie's office and told her that we would be out of the office for a while.

On the way to Al's house, I explained to Tracy that I thought it would be important to include Al in the planning. Knowing Baggy-D and Wendy like she did, Al could help us determine the best way to accomplish our goals.

Our ultimate goal was to infiltrate the Godfather's organization. But at that point, we had to be patient and wait to see what would happen as a result of our introduction to Baggy-D and Wendy.

I honked when we pulled into Al's driveway. The front door opened and she walked out wearing a pink sweat suit, black shoes, and a green hooded winter coat. She was carrying a large cup of pop. Her hair was unkempt and she hadn't put on any makeup. Tracy opened the car door and Al climbed into the backseat.

"How ya guys doing?" Al asked with a big smile.

Tracy told Al that we were having a productive day so far. I cracked open my window to get some fresh air circulating through the car. Tracy showed Al the pictures that we had picked up at the jail.

"Do you know who either one of these people are?" Tracy asked.

"That's Baggy-D and Wendy," Al quickly replied. "That's not a very good picture of Wendy. She must have had a bad night."

"We need to put our heads together and come up with a story that will help us gain their trust," I told Al.

Al smiled and said, "I've been thinking about that. I think that our best bet is to have Wendy take us over to the Godfather's house. I don't think we want to involve both of them. Besides, Wendy will take a liking to you right away.

"I think it would be best to keep Baggy-D out of it. Boy, he's a nut. He runs around a million miles an hour and he likes those guns."

"You've got a point," Tracy said. "But will you be able to cut Baggy-D out of it?"

"I'll just look him in the eye and tell him we don't have enough room for him in the car," Al said confidently. "He doesn't intimidate me!"

I told Al that I didn't want to have a fight break out. She assured me that it wouldn't be a problem.

Al thought that if Wendy was willing to go with us to the Godfather's house, Wendy could take me inside and introduce me to the Godfather. It would be an opportunity to begin building a relationship with him.

I told Al that she could continue to use the cover story about my being from southern Indiana. But she was not to go into detail about my family life or my farming business. Even though I had spent a great deal of my earlier days with my dad spraying chemicals on beans and corn and doing various other farm-related chores, I did not want to get in over my head.

Al asked us how soon before we could get started on our undercover work. I told her that first Tracy and I had to meet with our sergeant to get his approval. It might be that afternoon or it might take several days.

Al's body language clearly indicated that she was not happy with my answer. But it was the best answer I could give her. The sergeant would no doubt closely scrutinize every detail. If we didn't have all of our ducks in a row, the entire plan would be dumped.

Tracy reassured Al, "Hang in there. It will all come together soon. You're doing a great job so far!"

Al asked us if we had a few extra minutes to talk. When we said yes, she started to cry. She explained that she and her husband, Terry, were not getting along very well.

"Last night, he yelled at me again and told me I should not be helping you guys with this case. He said it was your job, not mine, to stop the Godfather," Al said.

"He told me that, if I wanted to help somebody, I should help him by getting a job. We're behind on our bills. Terry works at Danfort (a large meat processing plant in the Bottoms) and makes fairly good money. But, I don't know what he does with it because we never have any.

"I've got a bad back and can't work. I get bad headaches because of my back. I hope to use some of the money you are going to pay me for our bills."

I asked Al if Terry had ever hit her when they argued. She said that he had a bad temper, but only pushed her occasionally. She described him as thirty-five years old, Hispanic, 5 feet 10 inches tall, and weighing 175 pounds. Al said that Terry often came home drunk, as had happened the night before.

I asked Al to page me if she ever needed anything. She told me that she had already memorized my pager number. Tracy also told Al that she hoped that things would get better with Terry and to page her if I was ever unavailable.

"I'll call you as soon as we get the green light from our sergeant," I told Al. "In the mean time, take care of yourself."

Al leaned forward and gave Tracy a hug. Then, she reached over and hugged me. As she stepped out of the car, her familiar big smile had returned. We waved good-bye as we drove away.

When we got to the office, I asked Tracy if she would fill out the buy sheets, one for Baggy-D and Wendy and one for the Godfather.

I wanted to ask the sergeant if we could use the alternate undercover car, a white, 1978 Chevy Monte Carlo SS. It fit the circumstances better than my car. The alternate undercover car had been seized in an earlier drug investigation and had been in storage for about two years while the owner appealed the seizure. I would put dummy plates from a southern Indiana county on it to fit my cover.

The sergeant was not in the office. I asked Stephanie if she knew where he was. She said the only thing that he had told her when he left was that he would be available by pager. I didn't know what to think of it. Did he mean "don't call me" or "page me if you need something?"

Just then Tracy walked into Stephanie's office and said she was done with the paperwork. I told Tracy that I was going to page the sergeant to find out when he would be back in the office, then I wanted to go over the details again before he returned.

Several minutes later, Stephanie told me that the sergeant was on line two. He told me that he would not be back in the office at all that day. I explained that Tracy and I were ready to meet with him to discuss a possible buy with someone that might be able to introduce me to the Godfather. He said that it would have to wait until the next day. Both Tracy and I were disappointed that our case would have to wait until tomorrow.

I told Tracy that it would give us time to catch up on our paperwork, however. After she had returned to her office, I saw one of the outside lines light up. From the tone of her conversation, I knew that she was talking with Jason. I picked up my recorder and started to dictate the information that I had learned about Wendy.

I had almost finished the report when my pager went off. The number on my pager was Al's. I called her. She said that Terry had returned from work drunk. Al had told him that she was going to introduce me to Baggy-D and Wendy. Again, Terry had warned her not to get involved.

Al told Terry that it was important to her and she would not drop it. She explained to him that it was her way of setting things straight for what she had done while working for the Godfather. Al told him that if he didn't like the fact that she was helping us, he should keep his mouth shut and stop ragging on her.

Al said that Terry left the house after that and threatened not to come back. I asked her if she thought he meant it and she said no. Terry might be gone for a couple of days, but she thought he would return after he calmed down. She said a lack of money was the only problem she had when he left like that. I told her that the next day we might be able to arrange the buy from Baggy-D, then we would be able to pay her for her assistance.

After work I drove to Greenwood, a suburb of Indianapolis, to take my children out for dinner. My daughter was nine years old, and my son was six. It was my son's turn to pick a restaurant. My daughter suggested that he choose McDonalds, but he wanted to go to Pizza Hut. His choice made her upset. She whined that she didn't want to go to Pizza Hut.

I found their disagreement annoying. I remembered that when I was living at home with my parents, just getting the opportunity to go out to a restaurant was something special. My brother, sister, and I were happy to go out no matter where it was. Was it the changing times or was it something that I had done wrong as a parent?

I didn't see my children often enough, only every other weekend and maybe one other time in between. It was a big adjustment for me. Before my divorce, I was extremely involved in my children's lives. It saddened me when I realized how little time I spent with them anymore. I felt an overwhelming sense of loss because I no longer lived with them full time.

On the weekends when my children were with me, my stepchildren were also with us. They all got along fairly well despite the differences in their ages.

But at times, I thought that it was more difficult for my son to adjust to the new situation than it was for my daughter. My daughter was the oldest of the four children and had no problem being the leader. She was also the only girl. On the other hand, I could sense my son's pain when Nate and Joel would kiss me goodnight and tell me, "I love you."

Paula told me that I was being overly sensitive. She reminded me that Nate and Joel were also living away from their father, who lived in another state.

I knew what she was trying to say, but it didn't change the fact that I thought that her boys had it easier. Tom, her ex-husband, had remarried a woman who didn't have any children. So they didn't have to share their father with stepbrothers or stepsisters. And when Nate and Joel spent the weekend with their dad, they went back to the same house that they had lived in when their parents were married.

We all had adjustments to make in our lives. But it was a lot easier for me to understand what my own children were feeling than it was for me to try to understand what Paula and her children were experiencing. It was one of the reasons why my second marriage required so much effort and energy.

After dinner, I drove my children back to their home. My daughter asked me if Paula and I had anything planned for the following weekend, which is when my children would be with me next. I said, "Not yet, but I'm sure by then Paula and I will think of something special to do."

When I got home, Nate and Joel were playing downstairs and Paula was talking on the phone with one of her sisters. She smiled at me and continued on with her conversation. Paula spent most of her free time on the phone keeping up with what was happening in her home town. She had four sisters and many girlfriends who called with updates.

There was always something going on in her family. Between her sisters, four brothers, dad, stepmom, cousins, nieces, and nephews, life was like a soap opera.

The next morning, the sergeant said he could meet with Tracy and me right after the meeting.

I went to Tracy's office and warned her that the sergeant was not in a good mood. We went over our notes again so that we would be prepared.

During the morning meeting, we found out that no one was going to be too busy during the day that they couldn't break away from what they were doing to assist us with our attempted drug buy. Tracy and I told the other members of the unit about Baggy-D and Wendy and about all the information that we had gathered. Everyone appeared eager to help us with our investigation.

Tracy and I collected our notes and went to the sergeant's office. "Cross your fingers," I told her.

"It sounds like you've done your homework," the sergeant said as we walked into his office. "You shared some critical information during the morning meeting. Tell me your game plan for the proposed buy."

Tracy and I explained that Al would ride along with me to Baggy-D and Wendy's house on Olson. Al and I would go inside and Al would introduce me to them. She would tell them that I was in town for a short period of time and that I wanted to buy some cocaine.

If they had some to sell, she would ask them if it had come from the Godfather. Regardless of their answer, Al would insist that I wanted the good stuff. She would also let them know that I had a large customer base with the potential to make a lot of money if I could get hooked up with the Godfather's drugs. Al would suggest that we all go to the Godfather's house to buy some dope so that there would be no question of the quality.

Tracy told the sergeant that Al would cut Baggy-D out of the deal so that we would only have to be concerned with Wendy. Tracy also stated that, in her opinion, I would be able to control Wendy and use her to infiltrate the Godfather's organization.

I assured the sergeant that there would be enough support vehicles to follow me to Baggy-D's house, down to the Bottoms where the Godfather lived, and back to Baggy-D's house again.

Tracy handed the sergeant the buy sheets she had completed. After studying them for a few minutes, he looked up and told us to be careful. He warned us not to take any unnecessary chances. He asked me to brief him after we talked with Al.

Tracy and I left his office and hurried to call Al. After the fourth or fifth ring, she answered the phone. Al said that she was feeding her dogs. She sounded tired.

I asked her if her husband had come home the night before. She said that he had called her to see what she was doing, but that he didn't talk long. Al said she thought he probably had a girlfriend and was staying with her.

I asked Al if she had heard from either Baggy-D or Wendy since our last meeting. She said she hadn't.

"Tracy and I just talked with the sergeant and he gave us permission to meet with them," I told Al. "Will you call them and see if we can come over this morning sometime?"

"You bet!" she exclaimed. "What time do you want me to tell them we will be over?"

"Tell them that if I can get my chores done, we will be there around noon or so," I said.

I cautioned Al to be very brief during her conversation and to avoid answering any questions. Tracy told her to get something to eat and to call us after she had made contact with them.

Tracy made copies of the buy sheets while I asked the other members of the unit to meet us in the briefing room. I told the sergeant that I was waiting to hear back from Al, but that the buy was tentatively set up for noon. He said that he would rearrange his schedule so that he could be present.

Minutes later, Al paged me. She said that Baggy-D and Wendy were at home and that we could go over anytime after 10 a.m. Al wanted to know what she should wear. I told her she should wear what she normally wore.

"Just be yourself," I told her. "Do what you would normally do."

# Chapter 9

March 28, 1995, marked the beginning of the undercover phase of our investigation. With Al's help, it would be the starting point for several successful undercover investigations that would eventually lead to many more arrests and the convictions of several dangerous drug dealers in the Indianapolis area.

As the members of our unit assembled in the briefing room, I pulled the sergeant aside. I told him that I was concerned about the meeting with Baggy-D because of his alleged interest in guns.

"We need to be prepared for anything," I cautioned him.

"This is not going to be a free-for-all," he warned me. "You better be able to control the informant and the activities leading up to any possible buy or I will end the buy. If this becomes a cluster fuck, you'd better get the hell out of there."

Joe, David, Stuart, Tracy, Trish, and the sergeant were all present at the meeting. Tracy handed out copies of the buy sheets and pictures of Baggy-D and Wendy.

I started the briefing by explaining that Baggy-D and Wendy were believed to be associates of the Godfather. I described their connections to the Godfather, noting that the information came from Al. I said Al would introduce me to them as someone interested in buying cocaine. I said I hoped to use Wendy as an unknowing informant who would help me infiltrate the Godfather's operation.

Tracy added that Baggy-D was a cocaine, crack, and methamphetamine dealer known to mainline, and that he was believed to be a gun nut.

I informed everyone that Al would try to talk Wendy into riding with us to the Godfather's house at 1000 S.E. Lexington, Indianapolis, where we would attempt to buy cocaine. The other members of the unit knew this meant they'd have to follow us while we drove through the city from the north side of Indianapolis to the Bottoms.

Stuart asked us what would happen if Wendy would not take Al and me to the Godfather's house. Tracy said we might have to make a buy at the house on Olson in order to gain Baggy-D and Wendy's confidence.

Joe asked me what the rest of the unit should do if Wendy did take us to the Bottoms.

"The information that Tracy and I have gathered from various sources indicates that the Godfather often uses members of his organization to serve as security guards and lookouts at his house, and they're armed," I said. "Tracy and I did a drive by. We saw several small campers and trailers parked to the east of the Godfather's house. The security team occupies the campers. There are also people posted in the house at the upstairs windows."

"If they go mobile, don't loose Steve!" the sergeant said. "Once they get close to the Godfather's house, take a position where you won't burn them. Stay close enough so that you're in range of the repeater, but remember, they, too, have access to binoculars."

I told everyone that I would be satisfied if Wendy went into the Godfather's house by herself. But if at all possible, I wanted to accompany her when she went inside.

No matter what happened, I told them that I would feel safer if they kept their distance once I got close to the Godfather's house. I didn't want them to be too close to me. I wanted them just close enough to "maintain an eyeball," or to have a clear view of me at all times.

The last thing we went over was the danger signal I had chosen – Bear Lake. If for any reason I felt that there was a need to stop the undercover investigation, I would clearly state "Bear Lake" during my conversation. It would alert the members of the surveillance team to approach my location immediately with their guns drawn. They would be clearly identified as police officers because they would be wearing raid shirts or jackets, which had "Sheriff" printed on them. They would be responsible for securing the area and taking control of the people present.

By using the danger signal as part of a normal conversation, I could alert the surveillance team without tipping off the suspect. Hopefully, the team's approach and entry would be executed swiftly and safely in order to minimize the potential for injury to themselves, the suspect, and me.

Bear Lake is a casino near Chicago that I had visited a couple of times. It was critical that the danger signal be somewhat obscure so I wouldn't use it by mistake.

The sergeant asked if anyone had any questions. No one did; we were all focused and ready to go. He reminded us to check our gas gauges, then asked Joe to double-check the electronic listening device.

Tracy said that she would call Al while I searched my undercover car for anything that might indicate that I was a cop.

Joe was testing the repeater that he had just placed under the backseat of my car. He asked me to turn on my bug so that he could check the strength of the signal. I had chosen to use a bug that was disguised as a cell phone. I gave Joe a quick ten count. He gave me a "thumbs-up" from the surveillance vehicle indicating that the signal was at maximum strength. Next, I checked the microcassette recorder that I would be carrying. I replaced the battery and started to record. The playback indicated that it, too, was working properly.

I went back inside where Tracy was preparing the buy money that I would be using. David was in the process of recounting the $350. After recording the serial numbers of the bills, Tracy handed me the money. As was required by policy I again counted the money. I put some in my wallet and I put the rest in my front pants pocket.

The sergeant walked out of his office. "Is the bug working okay?" he asked.

"Yes," I replied.

"Have you checked your car yet?" he asked.

"Yes," I replied again.

"Do you have your gun with you?" the sergeant said.

I pulled out my stainless-steel Walther .380 caliber PPK from my waistband. I removed the magazine to show him that the gun was loaded.

He also made sure that I had the microcassette recorder, the buy money, my pager, and a full tank of gas. It didn't bother me to have the sergeant double-checking me as if I were a child leaving for the first day of school. Everything he was doing was for my protection. It was not a time to forget something that could potentially compromise the investigation or my life. He, too, had done undercover work and knew the importance of being prepared.

We all got into our vehicles for the final checks. The sergeant went through the roll call over the radios. We would each respond to our radio number after it was called. Next I turned on the bug and everyone else checked his or her monitors. I counted up to five and back down to zero. The sound of my voice was transmitted from the repeater to their monitors. It was a clear and strong signal. We were ready to go.

I took the lead as we left the parking lot. I was on my way to pick up Al. As I drove along, many different thoughts were running through my mind. *How would Al perform? Would Baggy-D be carrying a gun? Would Wendy come on to me a little too strong? Would Baggy-D be flying high on drugs? Could I successfully buy cocaine from Baggy-D? Would Al be able to resist using the drugs? What would the sergeant say if it turned out that Baggy-D and Wendy were not associated with the Godfather? Would I meet the Godfather today?*

As I always did before starting an undercover assignment, I said a short prayer to God, asking Him to protect me from harm and keep me safe. And because it was Al's first time working undercover as an informant, I asked Him to help her do a good job.

I pulled into Al's driveway and honked the horn. Tracy had followed me in her undercover car and was parked in the street about a half a block away. The other members of the surveillance team had pulled into a business parking lot several blocks away and were waiting for Tracy to radio them.

Within ten seconds, I saw Al walking out the front door. She was carrying a large plastic cup. She had a cigarette hanging from her mouth and she was wearing a pair of pants that were very tight. She had on a black leather motorcycle jacket similar to the one I was wearing.

As she got into my car, I noticed she didn't have a smile on her face and it seemed as though she had lost her excitement and enthusiasm. She was all business.

I wasn't sure what to make of her. It was as if she had become a different person. She was not talking a mile a minute and her body language was reserved. The tone of her voice was serious and quiet. Was she in a bad mood? Did she and Terry have another fight? Was Al feeling bad for promising something that she was not going to be able to deliver?

The only things that seemed to be the same as before were the huge cup of pop in her hand and the smell of her bulldogs on her clothes.

Al told me that Baggy-D had just called her and told her that he was going to be leaving soon. If we wanted to be sure to catch him at home, she suggested that we get going and not waste time sitting in her driveway talking. That was typical of most drug dealers. They sold drugs only when it was convenient for them or fit into their schedules. Many times we had to hurry up, then wait.

It was about twenty minutes from Al's house to Baggy-D's house on the north side of the city. Knowing that Tracy was listening to my conversation with Al, I said, "It sounds like we might find an empty house when we get there." Tracy would relay the information by radio to the other members of the surveillance team.

Al was not phased by the possibility of missing Baggy-D. Some informants in such a situation would get very upset and demand that we hurry so as not to miss our big chance. Al seemed to know that if this meeting with Baggy-D didn't take place as planned, there would be other opportunities.

At that moment, I recognized what was different about Al. She had become a part of her past. She was not pretending to be someone else like I was. She was the real deal. She was a confident, coolheaded, street-smart person with the determination to succeed in an illegal activity and not get caught.

As we backed out of Al's driveway and headed north, she told me she'd grown up in Indianapolis and had spent a lot of time with her father. He had been a fence, buying stolen property from a number of different thieves and reselling the items for a profit.

That environment had taught Al how to survive, earn a living, and avoid being arrested in the process. Over the years, Al had become acquainted with numerous criminals. She had built strong and lasting relationships with many of them. She had earned their trust and respect not only because of her association with her father, but also because she had committed several crimes herself.

Al confessed that what she was about to do would make her father turn over in his grave. But if she was going to live for Christ, she had to help dismantle the criminal organizations with which she was affiliated. In her mind, helping the police would repay God for her sins.

I listened closely as Al shared her experiences with me. I could sense that she was being sincere about wanting to change her life and live for Christ. I could feel the power of her words. I knew then that Al really did want to help us take down one of the largest drug dealers in Indianapolis. Time would tell if she would be able to accomplish her goal – a goal that was not too different from mine in many respects.

While we were having our conversation, Tracy radioed the other members of the surveillance team, who were following me as I drove to Baggy-D's house. The traffic was light. When I looked in my rearview mirror, I could see them.

I explained to Al exactly what we needed to accomplish when we met with Baggy-D and Wendy. She seemed to understand everything I was telling her. Because she was street-smart, Al was familiar with the information that I needed to gather in order to build a criminal case against the Godfather and his organization. I knew that she would be successful in assisting me with meeting my objectives. At the same time, I hoped she would share her criminal expertise with me.

My cell phone rang. It was Tracy. She said that Joe had driven past Baggy-D's house and couldn't tell if anyone was home. He did not see any cars parked in the driveway or in front of the house.

I asked Tracy to tell Joe to maintain eyesight of the house and report any movement.

As we got closer to Baggy-D's house, I asked Tracy to turn her headlights on and off if she was receiving a strong signal from the bug. I looked in my rearview mirror and saw her flash her lights. I slowed down a little and pulled out my microcassette recorder. I recorded a short lead at the beginning of the tape, then hid the recorder under my clothes.

Al looked at me and smiled, "It will be all right. The Lord will be with us."

"You're right," I said. "He will be."

I felt very comfortable being with Al. She seemed to be more relaxed and confident about what we were going to do than I was. She definitely did not act like it was her first time working as an informant.

As we turned the corner onto Olson, I saw the small yellow house. Just as Joe had reported, there were no cars nearby. I pulled up in front of the house and parked on the street. Al told me to sit in the car while she went to see if anyone was home.

I watched as she knocked on the front door. The blinds on the windows were pulled. The front door opened, but it was too dark in the house for me to see who answered the door. After a few seconds, Al turned away from the door and walked back to the car. I wondered what was going on. Someone inside the house closed the door.

Al reached for the passenger's door and got in. She said that Baggy-D and Wendy were home, and they wanted me to come in. Wendy had also asked that I park my car in the driveway instead of on the street. While I was moving my car, Al told me that there was a man she didn't know sitting on the couch.

After parking the car, Al and I walked up to the front door. Al had her glass of pop in her hand. The front door opened, and I saw a man that matched the picture that Al had shown me of Baggy-D. We stepped inside the darkened house. The only light in the living room came from the television.

The man looked at me and said, "Hey Bud, how ya doing? I'm Baggy-D."

Al introduced me as her friend Jack.

I said, "Hi," and quickly glanced around the room. I noticed a woman who appeared to be Wendy.

She motioned me in and asked, "Will you lock the door please?"

Al looked at Wendy with a puzzled expression on her face and said, "What?"

"Will you lock the door please?" Wendy repeated.

In all of my previous undercover experiences, no one had ever asked me to lock the door after I entered the house. As I reached out to lock the door, I noticed that a new deadbolt lock had been installed recently. I also noticed damage to the doorjam where somebody had obviously succeeded in forcing open the front door.

I did not feel comfortable locking the door behind me. What kind of message were they sending? I wondered how the members of the surveillance team were reacting. Were they frantically radioing back and forth trying to plan a strategy in the event that I would give the danger signal? How would they breach the locked front door without the assistance of a ram?

I was also concerned about how the sergeant would react to my decision to go ahead and lock the door instead of refusing her request to do so. Would he yell at me and insist that I should have questioned them? Would he tell me that I should have backed out of the deal if they had not agreed to keep the door unlocked? As in many instances in life, I had to make a split-second decision. My decision would be reviewed and judged by others who could take their time to consider the various advantages and disadvantages of locking the door.

I had no time for analysis. I decided to lock the door and not make a big deal out of it. It seemed to me that they were more fearful of someone else coming in unexpectedly than they were about my presence.

Baggy-D motioned for Al to follow him into another room. As they disappeared, I wondered what was going on.

I was left standing in the living room with Wendy and a tough-looking man sitting on the couch. He had shoulder-length brown hair and an unkempt beard. He wore a black leather coat, faded blue jeans, and black boots. He didn't utter a word. Instead, he stared at me, sizing me up. He had his right hand under his jacket at an angle, which indicated he was holding a gun.

The air in the room was heavy. Suddenly I felt uncomfortable, more uncomfortable than I ever felt on any other undercover assignment.

I could overhear their conversation from the next room.

Baggy-D asked, "Is this guy cool?"

"I wouldn't bring him here if he wasn't," Al replied.

"Well, he'd better be, because I'm not sure about him! I wasn't real happy with the last guy that I did business with that I didn't know!" Baggy-D said.

"You don't have to worry about this one. He's just a little old farm boy," Al joked.

Baggy-D asked, "Where does he live?"

"Between Ivy and Leon on a big farm. He has a real nice business going for him," Al said reassuringly.

Having completed his interrogation, Al and Baggy-D returned to the living room. The tension I had sensed when we entered the house suddenly subsided. I glanced at Baggy-D just as he was signaling to Wendy that everything was okay. Wendy smiled and started to joke around with Al. Baggy-D was more relaxed and, hopefully, ready to do business.

"So, you're from the southwestern part of the state?" Baggy-D said to me.

"No, it's pretty much straight south of here," I replied. "Where are you from?"

"Indianapolis, born and raised. But, been all over though," he said in a bragging tone. "I know people from all around, even in your neck of the woods!"

The small talk seemed to go on and on. I finally told Baggy-D that I needed to get going. Too much talking could get me into trouble. I didn't know what direction the conversation would go. I wasn't prepared, for example, to discuss topics such as the finer points of farming.

"We don't want to hold you up all day or anything. But we kind of wanted to sit around and talk for a little bit so that we could get to know you," Baggy-D said.

"Have you been down to the Godfather's lately?" asked Al.

"Why do you ask?" Baggy-D quickly responded with a hint of suspicion.

"I don't know. Just curious," Al said. "I haven't seen him for a day or two."

Baggy-D looked at me and said, "Al tells me that you want to buy a big chunk of cola."

"I can move a lot of shit down where I live, if the price is right," I said.

"Somewhere in the realm of $2,500 an ounce or in that area? Al said that you wanted me to show you how to cook it up?" His voice trailed off to the point where I couldn't understand what he was saying.

"Well, right now I just want to buy a little bit and try it out," I replied.

"That's good," Wendy said. "'Cause I would of wondered about you coming up here with a big wad of money and gambling it all on the first buy with us. I would have thought that you were a Fed or something."

All of us joined in as she laughed, except the man sitting on the couch.

Baggy-D said, "That's why all the questions. Okay? We wanted to know who we were dealing with."

I replied, "That's cool. I asked Al a bunch of questions about you before I came walking into your house with my hard-earned money."

"There's a lot of shit going on right now in Indianapolis," Wendy said. "A lot of people are getting busted."

"I've known him for five years now, right?" Al said as she looked at me.

"I don't want to be selling to the cops!" Baggy-D explained. His eyes were as cold as ice. He looked as if he were a serious businessman who didn't want to get busted.

"I've never been to jail, and I plan to never go to jail. I make mistakes like everybody else. But that is a mistake I will never make!" I proclaimed.

"I've been to jail before," Baggy-D confessed. "And, it's a place that I never want to go again!"

"Me either!" Wendy agreed.

"I can look right into a person's eyes and tell exactly where they're at. And you seem to be cool," Baggy-D stated with confidence.

"So what do you want? An eight ball (an eighth of an ounce)?" asked Baggy-D. "Or do you want two quarters?"

"You're going to get a better buy for an eighth," Wendy told me.

"How much for an eighth?" I asked.

"Oh, for you I'd do an eighth for around two and a quarter ($225). Your money is going to go a long way with our shit. You should be able to triple your money if you cut it right. Our stuff is fire! You know what I mean? You know what I mean?" Baggy-D said. "Our stuff is like a baseball. It will go a long ways. We don't cut our stuff. We don't have to to make money. It sells like hotcakes!"

"Do you want to get an ounce?" asked Baggy-D. "Or I could sell you a half for seven fifty ($750)."

I could tell that they felt more relaxed and that they wanted to make some money. Their greed was surfacing. They sensed that they could make some easy money selling to me. They were even dropping their price from $2,500 for an ounce of cocaine down to $1,500. I could hear the excitement in their voices. Baggy-D and Wendy were both talking at the same time. Wendy said that they had done some the night before, and it was good. They both continued to pitch their product just like car dealers trying to sell used cars.

"I think I'll just get an eighth this time. And if it's as good as you both say it is, I'm sure you'll be seeing me soon," I assured them.

"Great!" Baggy-D said quickly. "Sounds like a good deal. So how much money do you have on you?"

"I don't make a habit of sharing my finances or how much money I carry around with me with people I don't know," I said. "I will tell you I have enough on me to get the ball. I don't want you to think I was going to walk in here with $2,500 cash."

"We're not going to rob you or anything!" Wendy replied harshly.

"Just like you said, you didn't know him and he doesn't know you guys," Al said. "He didn't mean anything by it!"

"Well after this deal maybe we will all feel better about each other and things will go down with less of a hassle," Wendy said. "We didn't know how this would all go down today, so we don't have any right now."

"Yea," Baggy-D said. "How it works is, we go right to the main guy's house and get what we need. That way, there is no middleman or anything like that. We'll get the cola and meet you back here in an hour or so."

"We want to ride along with you," Al interrupted. "Then he could leave town right afterwards."

"Oh no!" Wendy replied angrily. "He won't go for that. I'm not going to take any strangers near there. He's been cracking down on that."

"We would sit out in the car," Al continued.

"No way," Baggy-D said. "That's not going to happen! You should know better than that Al."

"No, no way Al!" Wendy repeated. "He'll step on me."

"Don't you trust me?" Al asked.

"It's not that. It's no new people around there," Wendy said. "It's his rule, not ours."

Al understood our goals and what we needed to accomplish on the buy. I wanted to build a strong case against the Godfather and to do that I needed a hand-to-hand buy, an act he could not defend in court.

So Al continued to push them for more than they were offering.

"I'll go with her," Baggy-D said, pointing to Al. "And you stay here with her." He pointed to Wendy.

"I'm from a small town," I said. "We do things a little different down there."

"You'll be here in my house with my lady, okay? And I'm with her, your lady, okay? Right?" Baggy-D said.

"No. She's my friend, not my lady," I insisted. "And without knowing you, the last thing I would want to do is be here alone in your house with your lady."

"Oh, I'm sorry. Is that what you meant? That's cool. You don't think it would be cool for you and I to be together alone with Baggy-D not here," Wendy said.

"I see," said Baggy-D. "Okay. I can't take you to the house. But how about Al and I dropping you and my lady off at a restaurant or a bar nearby. You guys can have a drink. And then we'll stop back and pick you up after we get the stuff? Then you can head out of town. Five minutes and we'd be right back. Okay?"

"Yeah, I like that idea. That would be okay wouldn't it?" asked Wendy. "That way you wouldn't feel so uncomfortable being alone here at the house with me. That way no one gets hurt." She laughed as if it was every man's dream to be alone with her. "I love that!"

"I'm not trying to offend you," I said to Wendy. "But I guess I'm from the old school."

"No, that's okay. I like that in a man," Wendy said.

The phone rang. While Baggy-D answered the phone, I told Wendy that I wanted to speak with Al outside.

Al followed me to my car. Once inside the car, I told Al and the surveillance team members who were monitoring the bug what I thought about Baggy-D's suggestion.

If at all possible, I wanted to drive one of them to the Godfather's house. Then I could watch Baggy-D or Wendy go in and come back out with cocaine. I wanted Al to convince them that mine was a better plan. If she were unsuccessful, I would end the meeting and come back some other time after having the opportunity to speak with the sergeant.

Al asked me if I had noticed the guy on the couch and what he was holding in his hand. I said I had seen him and that it appeared to me that he was armed. She said she had seen the gun in his waistband before I entered the house. Al referred to him as their watchdog, but said she'd never seen him before. She also pointed out that there was no indication in the house that they dealt drugs. They had put away their scales and bags. For some reason, they were being really careful.

We decided Al needed to go back inside. She gave me the "thumbs-up" just before the door opened. It was about seven to ten minutes before I saw the front door open again. Al walked out by herself. I thought to myself, *I guess I asked too much of Al, especially since this was the first time we were working undercover together.*

When Al got into the car she winked at me. "I did it," she said with confidence. "Wendy will be right out."

Al told me that Baggy-D talked a good talk. Wendy, however, was the one with the connection to the Godfather. Wendy had been his best prostitute.

Before Wendy came outside, I told Al that if Wendy wouldn't take me inside to meet the Godfather, Al should try to go inside with her. That way, Al would have control of the money. And if the deal went smoothly, the Godfather might be willing to let me come in the next time.

I asked Al if Wendy carried a gun. She said that Baggy-D wouldn't let her. Wendy wanted to but, since she was such a hothead, he didn't trust her with one.

"She might want to take the money and go with him into his office and do the deal without me. That's where he does his business. Is that all right?" Al asked.

"That's fine. Just stay as involved as he will let you," I told her.

"It looks like we're going to do it," Al said. "I mean we're actually going to do it. We're going to get inside!" She sounded excited.

I told her that she was doing a great job, that I was proud of what she was doing not only for me, but also for the community. We all wanted to get rid of the drugs in our neighborhoods.

I gave Al $300 to buy cocaine from the Godfather. While she was counting the money, Wendy walked outside. Al finished counting just as Wendy opened the car door.

"Nice car," Wendy said as she climbed into the backseat.

Wendy was dressed as if she were going to work. She had on tight jeans, a tight blouse unbuttoned low enough to expose most of her breasts, a cheap fur coat, and cheaper perfume.

She giggled and talked nonstop. She said something to me about putting on my seat belt as she leaned forward to get closer to me.

I told her that I always wore my seat belt. "I don't want to give the cops an excuse to stop me," I said jokingly.

"Yeah, he's pretty cautious," Al added.

I let Wendy tell me how to get to the Godfather's house. I acted as if I didn't know the streets of Indianapolis. We were driving from the near north side of Indianapolis to the south side. It was going to take us about twenty minutes to get there.

I repeated the streets aloud as Wendy told me where to turn. It helped the surveillance team to keep up with us as the various vehicles attempted to blend in with the traffic. It also allowed them to follow at a safe distance so as not to be detected. Wendy was looking all around as we were driving. She would even look behind us occasionally.

From her constant chatter, I guessed that she was high. Working undercover with someone who was using could be unpredictable and dangerous. I knew I needed to be prepared for anything.

Along the way, Wendy said, "Give me the money, now. I don't want to be handling money once we get there."

"I already got it," Al responded.

Wendy went back to her rambling. Occasionally Al and I would get in a word here or there. But for the most part, Wendy went from one topic to the next without missing a beat. The twenty-minute drive seemed to be taking an eternity.

Then Wendy started to hit on me. She asked me if I was married. When I said that I was, she laughed and said that it didn't matter to her. She whispered to Al, "You know Al, your friend's pretty cute!"

She started calling me "Honey." At one point, she leaned over the front seat and suggested that we do something later, hinting that I would have a great time.

As we got closer to the Godfather's house, Wendy told Al to give her the money.

"Why?" I asked.

She said that Al would have to wait in the car with me. She would run inside and be back out in a minute.

Al told Wendy that I was a little leery of giving money to a woman that I had just met.

Wendy replied, "I'm not like that. I'm not about taking people's money and running off. Quit worrying! Will you stop worrying? You worry too much. Come on. Your money is safe with me. I'm not taking your shit. Okay? I'm not about that. I don't have to do that. I make too much money to do stupid shit like that."

"Well," I hesitated.

"Come on. Give me the money and I'll be back with your dope!"

"Okay. Give her the money," I said to Al.

Wendy grabbed the money and put it in her pants pocket. Then she told me to pull off the road and park the car. We were still about a block from the Godfather's house. Wendy told me to wait for her. She jumped out of the car and started walking in the direction of the Godfather's house.

I had tried my best to get Al to go with Wendy, but I didn't want to push it. No one had ever gotten this close to the Godfather before. I could only hope that the sergeant wouldn't be too upset with me because I had given Wendy the money. He always said that if you let someone out of your sight with the money, there was a good chance that they would go in the front door and right out the back door. I trusted that that was not going to be the case with Wendy.

I told the surveillance team that Al and I were waiting in the car while Wendy went inside. I also told them that I was going to move closer to the house so that I could watch Wendy come out. That allowed the surveillance team to keep their distance. I would make up an excuse for my actions later if Wendy questioned me.

Soon Wendy came out of the house and got into an older, gray-colored pickup truck. She talked with the female driver for a few minutes, then went back inside the house.

A few minutes later, Wendy came out of the house again; this time she started walking to where I had let her out of the car. She glanced in our direction but continued to walk the other way. I could only guess why she was walking away from us. So, I pulled out onto the street and drove past her, watching her in my rearview mirror. I stopped the car in the same spot where I had first dropped her off.

She opened the door and climbed into the backseat. She told me to wait a minute, that the Godfather didn't have any drugs but that we were still in luck. Suddenly, an old beat-up pickup truck pulled up next to us. An attractive young woman was driving.

Wendy told us that the driver was a friend of hers and that if I followed the truck for a short distance, her friend would score some cocaine for us.

I decided not to proceed any further. Everything had to stop. It was time to "nut" the deal. Buying from Wendy's friend wouldn't be making progress in our attempt to build a case against the Godfather. At the very least, Wendy had not run out the back door with my money.

"What's going on?" I said to Wendy.

She shouted, "Follow her! Follow her!"

"Slow down," I said. "First of all, I want my money!"

She continued to yell, "Follow her! Follow her! She lives right down the street. I can get some from her." She pulled the money from her pocket. "Your money is right here," she said.

I tried to remain calm. "I want my money!" I said firmly.

Wendy continued to demand that we follow her friend and that we buy the drugs at her friend's house. She insisted that we get moving in order to catch up with the truck.

"That is my money and I will be the one to decide where I spend it!" I said. "I'm in charge of what we do!"

"Just relax. I know what's going on!" Wendy said.

"Give me the money!" I demanded angrily, and I reached back and grabbed it from her.

She looked surprised, but I didn't care what she thought.

"Wow!" she exclaimed as she leaned back against the seat. The street girl who was used to getting what she wanted didn't know what to say. For the first time since getting into the car at Baggy-D's house, she was quiet.

After a few moments of silence, I said, "I've got to get going. Let's do this some other time when I don't have to run all over Indianapolis."

I started driving back to Baggy-D's house. We had made an attempt, had spent a lot of time, and had no drugs to show for it.

I questioned Wendy, "I thought this source of yours could get whatever dope you wanted? I guess maybe he's not that big after all if he doesn't even have an eighth on hand."

Wendy answered, "He's just out right now. If we come back later, he'll have more."

"I just spent half a day driving up to Indianapolis for nothing!" I said.

"If we had followed my friend, we would have scored," she said.

"I could have scored from someone closer to my home," I said. "But I was told that the Godfather had the 'fire' – the best stuff in Indianapolis. And I thought this deal had been set up by phone before we had even left your house."

"I thought it was, too. He goes through a lot of shit and he runs out fast," Wendy said. "It's a matter of timing. You guys came at a different time than we thought you were coming. And by the time we got down there, he was out. It's not that big of a deal, really."

"We saw you come out of the house, get into the pickup with that girl, and then go back inside the house. He thought you were working for the cops," Al interjected.

"Look, I work in an escort service," Wendy yelled at us. "I am not a cop. Don't be stupid. The man runs out fast. That's all there is to it! When Al called at 9 o'clock, we set it up for 10 a.m. And, you didn't show up when we thought you would."

"I'm not interested in your excuses," I told Wendy. "I want to be able to come into town whenever I want to, drop in and pick up some dope. I was told that you could carry me, but I guess you can't help me!"

"That's not what I understood," Wendy said. "From now on, we won't have to travel. They will have someone deliver it to us."

"I just don't have a good feeling about this situation," I said.

She pleaded with me, "Give us another chance!"

"Al's got my phone number," I said. "You can reach me through Al."

I dropped Wendy off at Baggy-D's. I was disappointed that things had ended like they did. I had had high hopes of getting my foot in the door of the Godfather's organization. However, there was one positive result from the attempted buy. Al had done a wonderful job as an informant, better than any other informant I had ever worked with.

I dropped Al off at her house and told her to call me if she heard from Baggy-D or Wendy. Then I headed back to the office. Maybe I had relied too heavily on the assumption that I could get close to the Godfather through Baggy-D and Wendy.

We all met back at the office. Tracy and the other members of the unit were pleased with their surveillance efforts. Like me, they, too, were disappointed that we had been unable to purchase any cocaine. They agreed that I made the right decision not to make a drug buy from the unknown female in the pickup truck. The sergeant didn't really have anything to offer. He sat quietly while the unit discussed the attempted buy.

# Chapter 10

Later that day, I received a page from Jake, an informant. In the past, Jake had provided a lot of valuable information. I called him back. He sounded as excited as he could be.

Jake told me that on March 26th at approximately 7 p.m., he and several other people had gone to a house near S.E. 11th and Maury. He said that a man known as the Godfather ran a big drug operation out of the house. One of his companions, Micky Butts, had gone into the house to buy some crack. The rest of them sat outside in the car waiting for Micky. After a few minutes, Jake had gotten impatient and had gone inside to see what was taking so long.

When he entered the house, he was stopped by several men armed with what he thought were Mac-10 machine guns. There were several Hispanic men, a Black man, and several White men standing in the kitchen. Jake said that as he entered the kitchen, one of the Hispanic men used a blanket to cover up a huge pile of plastic bags filled with a powdered substance. One of the armed men instructed him to turn around and leave the house. Jake said that he did what he was told and quickly.

Moments later, Micky returned to the car with some crack cocaine. Jake described the Godfather as a White man in his late forties to mid-fifties.

I told Tracy about the phone call and asked her if she wanted to meet with Jake. I explained to her that I had played dumb and wanted Jake to show me the house. So, we met Jake at S.E. 14th and Maury. He described the house and how to get there. We followed his directions and, sure enough, he led us directly to the Godfather's house. We had another source that could confirm that the information we had gathered was correct.

Tracy asked Jake if he would keep his ears open and let us know what was going on at the house. Jake said that he would.

Very little was said around the office about our "no go" with Baggy-D and Wendy. I guess my expectations were higher than those of my co-workers. Instead of looking at the glass as half empty, maybe I should have been looking at the glass as half full.

After washing the dinner dishes that evening, my pager vibrated. I recognized the number as Al's home phone number. Instead of dropping everything, I continued to clean up the kitchen. Soon, my pager was vibrating again.

Once again the digital readout flashed Al's phone number. Then, my pager vibrated again.

I walked downstairs to the basement so that Nate and Joel wouldn't interrupt me. While I was dialing Al's number, my pager vibrated. I cleared it without even looking at the number. When I dialed the last number, there was a busy signal. She must have been on the phone calling me.

I pushed the redial button. The phone rang once and Al answered.

"I've been trying to reach you," Al explained. "We're in. We're in."

"What do you mean, 'we're in'?" I asked.

"I ran into Yvonne, Marcus' girlfriend. We're supposed to pick her up at 8 o'clock tomorrow morning. She will ride along with us over to the Godfather's house and take us inside to buy some crack," Al replied.

"That's great news," I said.

"This time we'll buy some dope," Al said confidently.

I told Al that I would have to run it past the sergeant first. I would have to verify Yvonne's identity before I could even consider talking with the sergeant. Al told me that identification wouldn't be a problem because Yvonne had been arrested several times for prostitution by the Indianapolis Police Department.

Al said, "I think there is a warrant for her arrest right now. She is Black, about twenty-five years old, 5 feet 4 inches tall, weighs 140 pounds, and has brown hair and brown eyes. Yvonne lives with Marcus in the 2600 block of Lay Street in Indianapolis."

Al told me that Yvonne was a prostitute who worked with the Godfather's modeling service. Al also said that Yvonne had quite a temper.

I explained to Al that I would not be in the office until around 7:30 the next morning. There was no way that we would be able to keep an 8 a.m. appointment. "If things go well, we might make it sometime around 10 a.m.," I said.

She told me to get a good night's sleep because the next day was the day she had been anticipating. "I'm going to take down the Godfather and destroy all of the terrible things he stands for," Al said.

Following Al's call, I was excited. Then I remembered that just twenty-four hours prior, I had thought we were going to get into the organization with Wendy's help. Maybe I needed to slow down. I shouldn't expect too much from our meeting with Yvonne. And besides, I still needed to learn enough about her to get the sergeant's permission to set up a meeting.

That night, I did more thinking than sleeping. I wondered what might happen. *Would Yvonne turn out to be just like Wendy – someone who would take my money and come out of the house empty-handed? Would she take me with her, only to be turned away? What type of security system would the Godfather have in place that I might have to pass through? Would the Godfather's lookouts spot the surveillance team? Would I have to answer a lot of questions in order to prove myself to the Godfather? Would I be asked to use the drugs in order to prove myself?*

These and many other questions filled my mind. I could feel my heart rate quicken. I was getting hot as I lay in bed. As more thoughts came and went, I could feel the sheets getting damp. I was breaking out in a sweat. There were so many things that could go wrong. Yvonne might refuse to introduce me to the Godfather or, even worse, there might be gunfire! How many of the things we'd heard about the Godfather and his organization were true and how many were just myths?

The next morning, March 29, 1995, I went into the office a little earlier than normal. I had a lot of information to verify before I could meet with the sergeant. When I checked the Department of Transportation (DOT) files, I learned that there was in fact a woman named Yvonne A. Jametta. Her date of birth was January 2, 1968. The DOT described her as a Black woman with brown eyes, 5 feet 4 inches tall, and weighing 145 pounds.

The address did not match, but the license had been issued five years earlier. Because it was common for people to move and not update their address with the DOT, this did not surprise me.

Next I ran a check to see if there were any warrants for her arrest. The printer readout read "Wanted Person." I thought to myself, *Your information appears to be correct, Al.* The first warrant was for misdemeanor theft; bond was set at $130. There was a second, more serious, warrant for three counts of felony forgery and failure to appear; bond was set at $10,000.

Even after having verified her identity and having confirmed Al's statement that there was a warrant for Yvonne's arrest, I still had to confirm that the address she had given me on Lay Street belonged to either Yvonne or Marcus Morrill.

I called my contact at the utility company. I asked her who was registered for service at 2600 Lay Street in Indianapolis. I was not surprised when she replied, "Marcus Lester Morrill." The Social Security numbers he had provided when he had applied for service matched the number I had from his criminal record.

I also asked her who was listed for service at the house just west of 2600 Lay Street. She replied that Jay Daniel Swartz was the customer at 2562 Lay Street.

Al had told me that a husky, bald, White man in his mid-thirties lived next to Marcus and Yvonne. She had said that the man went by the name Big Jay. I used the information the power company had provided and I learned from DOT files that a Jay Daniel Swartz had a valid license with an address of 2562 Lay Street.

The physical description in the DOT records matched the description Al had given me of Big Jay. In reviewing his criminal record, I learned that he had two arrests for assaulting police officers, one for resisting arrest, and one for prostitution. Al had said that Big Jay's role in the Godfather's organization was helping with the escort service. He drove the prostitutes to their calls and provided security for them.

In a short period of time, I was able to confirm all the information Al had given me on the phone the night before. I could hear the other members of the unit arriving at work. As Tracy walked by my office, I motioned for her to come in.

She was excited to hear about Al's latest information. However, she was cautious about the possibility of getting an introduction to the Godfather through Yvonne. "But it's worth a shot," Tracy said.

Tracy helped me put a buy sheet together and set up a travel plan. While she was working, I went to the sergeant's office. He was reading the morning paper. The sergeant looked up from the paper and said, "What ya got?"

He was pleased with the legwork I had already completed. I explained that Yvonne Jametta had a felony warrant for her arrest. I was hoping he wouldn't say that we were compelled to arrest her instead of using her to get to the Godfather.

The sergeant said to put the information about her warrants on the back burner and see where we could get by using her as an unwitting informant. "If for some reason she doesn't work out, you can use the warrants as leverage to get somewhere," he suggested.

After going over the details and outlining our intended travel route, the sergeant approved the buy attempt. He never said anything about our failed attempt with Wendy. I think the sergeant appreciated my perseverance and my continued search for ways to get into the organization. To me, the case was worth the extra time and effort I was putting into it. I did, however, realize that much of the credit belonged to Al.

I stopped by Joe's office, where he was meeting with Stuart, and asked Joe if he could get the equipment ready for a mobile undercover buy. I briefly explained what our objective was so that he would know what equipment was needed.

Stuart volunteered to take the money out of the safe and record the serial numbers.

With everyone's help, we started the pre-buy meeting without any delays. My meeting with Yvonne was going to be very similar to the attempt I had made with Wendy the previous day. The objective was the same – to use an unwitting informant to help me infiltrate the Godfather's organization.

The only differences were the names of the informants and their addresses. I would still be the undercover officer working with Al and the informant. As simple as our objective was, we were all aware of the possible roadblocks that we might encounter and the potential dangers.

I called Al and told her that Tracy and I were on our way to pick her up. After picking up Al, we met the surveillance team in a nearby grocery store parking lot. Tracy switched over to another car. I turned on my electronic listening device to check the signal strength. Joe gave me the "thumbs-up."

After the surveillance team left the parking lot, the sergeant motioned for me to come closer. He reminded me that I needed to be careful and I needed to think before I acted. "Don't get in over your head," he said. "It's just another drug deal. We all want to go home afterward. The more time you spend inside the Godfather's house, the higher the risk!"

We headed off to 2600 Lay Street. Along the way, Al told me what cars might be parked at the house on Lay Street. Through my electronic listening device, I repeated the information for the surveillance team. Just like the day before when we picked up Wendy, Al was very relaxed. I was more nervous than she seemed to be. I had participated in many other undercover operations and Al was only on her second undercover assignment. Why was I feeling like a rookie and why was she acting like a professional?

As we turned off of S.E. 25th and onto Lay Street, Al pointed to a small, one-story white house. One of the cars Al had described was parked outside of Big Jay's house. I informed the surveillance team that we were seconds away from arriving at our intended destination, the house at 2600 Lay Street. I turned on the microcassette recorder and hid it under my clothes.

As we approached Marcus' house, Al identified the two men standing next to an old black and yellow car parked in the driveway at 2562 Lay Street as Big Jay and Marcus. Both men watched as I parked the car at the end of the driveway. I couldn't tell if they were going to come over or if they were going to stay away.

Al warned me that Marcus carried a gun and was very quick to use it. She also cautioned that Big Jay could "lay you out" with one punch. I hoped that they would keep their distance while I waited for Al to get Yvonne. Al left the car and immediately went inside the house. I wondered whether Yvonne would agree to come with us without hesitation or would Al have to spend some time convincing her to come along.

I didn't have to wait very long. The front door of the house opened. Al and Yvonne appeared. Yvonne walked over to the two men in the driveway. After a brief conversation with them, Yvonne walked to the car with Al. Al opened the passenger side door and let Yvonne get in first. Yvonne made eye contact with me. She smiled and sat down in the backseat.

While Al was introducing me to Yvonne, I turned the car around in the driveway. The two men were still watching us. I nodded to them in respect as we pulled away from the house. I was thankful that I didn't have to interact with them. From what Al had said, it wouldn't have been unusual for them to initiate a confrontation.

On the way over to the Godfather's house, my mind wandered, *Will it be the same as yesterday? Maybe today will be the start of something big.* So many things raced through my mind. I tried not to think about the potential danger that I might encounter.

Al and Yvonne were talking about anything and everything – the escort service, Yvonne and Marcus's relationship, and many other topics that didn't pertain to me. I was glad to be left out of their conversation. Besides, I don't think I could have gotten a word in edgewise. They were both talking a mile a minute. It made for an interesting ride. On the one hand, it seemed to take forever because I had to listen to them carrying on and on. But on the other hand, the ride seemed to end before it started.

As we turned the corner at S.E. 10th and Lexington, I noticed a lot of people milling around outside of the Godfather's house. I parked the car along the side of the road. There were about eight other cars parked on both sides of the street and in the driveway. There were also two campers parked in the yard.

Al opened her door and stepped out. She pulled the seat forward so that Yvonne could get out. Suddenly, Yvonne declared, "I'm not going in."

Al asked, "Why not?"

"Because I don't want any part of this!" Yvonne insisted.

I looked at Al. I thought, *Here we go again. This is going to be a repeat of yesterday's experience with Wendy. Why did Yvonne agree to drive all the way over here and, then, decide not to take us inside?*

I told Al, "Well, I guess we might as well take her home and forget it."

Al was upset but determined, "I guess I'll have to take you inside myself."

"Are you sure?" I said.

"You never know unless you try," Al said.

Yvonne turned away from me and mumbled under her breath, "I wouldn't if I were you."

I was beginning to get a little concerned. What did she mean?

Al looked at me and asked, "Are you coming?"

I took the keys out of the ignition, got out of the car, and shut the door.

I hoped we had given the members of the surveillance team enough time to get in position. They wouldn't get too close but at least one of them had to be able to see me. I wondered if their hearts were beating as fast as mine.

They had a lot of responsibility resting on their shoulders. They had to be ready to come running if I gave the danger signal. Not only was my safety at risk, but theirs was as well.

The person under the most pressure out of all of us was the sergeant. He called the plays. Like a quarterback in an important game, the sergeant would get all of the glory if things went well and we were successful. But if anything went wrong, fingers would be pointed at him. I knew that was why he leaned on me so hard.

A situation such as this one required a leader that had extensive experience. The sergeant was well qualified for the job. If I could have picked anyone to supervise the unit and watch my back, it would have been him.

Several people standing around outside the house recognized Al. She walked up to one guy and gave him a hug. I stayed a step behind her as we made our way toward the two-story, multicolored house.

I still couldn't get over how the siding color varied because of the numerous additions that had been made to the house. And, it was odd how the windows had been pieced together from various types of buildings. It was obvious that union workers had not constructed the additions. The cost to complete the additions had to have been minimal. And besides, the design was unconventional.

Al yelled at a man who was walking away from the house, "Hi Robert! Where you going?" I recognized him. It was Robert Porter, the Godfather.

"I came to visit you and I brought a friend with me," Al said quickly as we approached him.

The Godfather didn't acknowledge my presence. "I was just leaving for a while," he replied. "I've got some things in town I want to get done."

"How long are you going to be?" Al asked. "I was hoping to talk with you."

"I'll be back shortly," he answered. "Anna is inside if you want to visit with her."

The Godfather turned and walked away from us. He didn't seem to be very receptive to our visit. He spoke with a deep, dull voice and a slight accent. During his brief conversation with Al, I got the impression that he hadn't had much of an education.

At that point, I was within reach of the Godfather. That type of person had a certain air about them. I sensed it in him. I had heard many stories about people like the Godfather. I had heard stories firsthand from people who knew and feared the Godfather. The facts and the fiction concerning Robert Porter had blended together to create a mystique. He was considered untouchable.

As I watched him walk away, I thought that any chance I might have had of continuing with the investigation was suddenly gone. Our intentions were good but the opportunity just wasn't there. Was it to be the final attempt of the investigation? My encounter with the Godfather had ended without so much as an introduction.

PRISON BOOK PROJEC
P.O. Box 1146
Sharpes, FL 32959

# Chapter 11

Al turned back toward me and said, "Let's go inside. I'll introduce you to Anna."

I was feeling disappointed that we had come so close only to have the Godfather give us the cold shoulder. I felt that anything else we might do would simply be a waste of time. I thought the surveillance team might also be feeling let down. The sergeant was probably already turning his attention to something else.

"What the heck," I responded. I followed Al to the back door of the old, rundown house. She opened the screen door and stepped inside the enclosed porch.

While my eyes were adjusting to the change in lighting, I heard Al say, "Morning, Anna."

When my eyes had finally adjusted to the darkness, I saw four women of various ages sitting around an old kitchen table. It was a Formica table like the ones used by people when I was growing up in the 1960s. They were drinking out of coffee cups. I walked up two steps and into the kitchen, stopping next to Al.

I quickly surveyed the room. It appeared that the women had not been up very long. There were cigarettes burning in several ashtrays. Three of the women were wearing robes; the fourth woman had on jeans and a brown sweater. There were dirty dishes on the counter and in the sink. The inside of the house didn't look any better than the exterior.

I thought to myself, *This is the home of one of the biggest and most dangerous drug dealers in Indianapolis?* It looked more like a crack house than the home of someone making thousands of dollars dealing in illegal drugs, running a prostitution service, and fencing stolen goods. I didn't see anything of value as I looked around the porch and the kitchen.

Al went over to an empty chair and sat down. I followed her lead and took a seat. We had obliviously interrupted an intense conversation between the woman who was dressed and the woman Al had addressed as Anna. The woman wearing jeans wiped tears from her eyes, and then stormed from the room as we joined them.

Al introduced me to Anna as Jack, her farmer friend from southern Indiana.

Anna said, "Hello," then started to tell Al about an event that had occurred several days before. It was about something completely unrelated to our undercover investigation – just small talk between two friends. Their conversation lasted for about fifteen minutes.

I was beginning to think that it was all a waste of time. They weren't discussing anything pertaining to our investigation, and Anna was simply ignoring me. I began considering how I could tell Al that we needed to get going.

Finally, Al said to Anna, "Can you help out my friend?"

Anna's response was quick, "No, there's nothing going on around here."

That was it? Anna had made it very clear that she did not want to have anything to do with me. She continued to smoke. Her long brown hair was unkempt and it looked to me as if she had not taken off her makeup from the day before.

I didn't feel welcome and decided it was time to say good-bye. I looked at my watch. We had been in the house for about twenty-five minutes.

Suddenly, the back door opened and closed. I could hear male voices. The Godfather entered the kitchen. Three men were with him. The Godfather said hello to Al and sat down at the table. Several minutes passed with only small talk.

Al turned to me, "You sure have been quiet, Jack."

"I'm still not feeling the best after last night's partying," I replied. I held my hand up to show them that it was shaking. It wasn't an act, though it wasn't from drinking the previous night either. I was shaking because of the dangerous situation I was in.

After several minutes, Al asked the Godfather if she could talk with him in his office. They stood up and walked out of the kitchen. Not waiting to be invited, I followed them down the hallway and into the office. After entering the small room, I closed the door behind me.

The Godfather sat down in a chair behind the desk. I sat down next to Al on an old green-colored couch. Behind the couch, there was an open closet. As I surveyed the room, I saw a camouflage, canvas, rifle gun case leaning against the wall near the desk. There was obliviously something in it.

Several feet from the desk, there was an unusual stand that held several large assault-type knives, any one of which could have caused a great deal of serious injury, or even death, if used on a person. They were not your typical buck knives. I couldn't think of any reason, sporting or other wise, for having weapons like these except for the purpose of hurting someone or something.

Al and the Godfather continued their small talk for several more minutes. During that time, my mind wandered. It appeared that, maybe, we were finally going to get somewhere. Were things falling into place or was I just getting my hopes up? Up to that point, the only thing I had witnessed was several people involved in what I would consider boring conversations. By no means had I heard or seen anything that could have been considered illegal.

Then, to my surprise, the Godfather looked at me and asked, "What do you want?"

Al looked at me as she responded, "You want some crank and crack. Right?"

I tried to answer her. I had to clear my throat first. "Yeah, if you got any?"

"Not right now," the Godfather replied.

What a roller-coaster ride! Why did he ask me what I wanted if he didn't have anything to offer?

Al asked him, "Robert, you remember me telling you about my buddy Jack, don't you? He's the farmer guy from southern Indiana."

He replied, "Yeah, I think so. What brings you up to the big city? Isn't that a long drive?"

I suddenly found myself immersed in my role. "The only crank they seem to have down where I live is that bathtub shit," I said. "When I've come up to Indianapolis, I've been able to pick up some good stuff. But I really don't like making that many trips up to Indianapolis, then having to transport the shit back home. Al told me that she had a good friend in Indianapolis who might be able to sell me large quantities of great stuff. I could make fewer trips to Indianapolis and be more profitable."

"She did, did she?" the Godfather asked. "Well there's nothing going on around here now."

"Tell him about the cocaine," Al said to me.

"There is an increased demand for crack down home, too. But, I don't know how to turn it hard from the powder," I said.

"I told him you were the best cooker around," Al said to the Godfather. "Can you teach him how to rock it up?"

The Godfather said, "Well, I guess I learned from the best teacher around. And now, the student is better than the teacher!"

"Al said that you're the best," I said, hoping to stroke his ego.

"When I get done, there ain't no waste leftover," he bragged. "If I use a quarter ounce of powder, my finished product turns out to be a quarter ounce of rock."

"Sounds like you were right, Al," I said.

"You can't buy any better duff (crack cocaine) than what I make," he said. "If you get stopped with powder, that gets you ten (10 years in prison). But if you get caught with duff, that will get you twenty-five (25 years in prison). And, you don't want to be looking at that!"

The window of opportunity was opening up. We were talking about drugs. Maybe I could get the Godfather to tell me incriminating stories about his experiences with drugs and about the other things he was involved in. He seemed to be letting his guard down. It was like two fishermen bragging about their fishing experiences.

I did not want to portray myself as a successful dealer. Instead, I wanted to appreciate how successful he had become. I wanted to bait him into thinking that my dreams were those of becoming even half as successful as he was. I would act like a student and hope that he would take the role of the teacher.

"I'm concerned about getting pulled over for no reason when I drive back home from Indianapolis with dope," I said. "Do you have any suggestions on how I might better transport the dope back home?"

"If you're going to have a girl riding along with you, have her stick it up inside her (in her vagina)," he said. "That way, you don't get busted. That will just make her want to have sex with you more."

Then the Godfather yelled out, "Anna, come here!" He turned to me and asked, "How much do you want to buy?"

"Either a couple hundred dollars worth or, maybe, an eight ball," I said, leaving the door open for him to make a suggestion. He started quoting me his prices. "I'll sell you an eight ball for $250 or quarter ounce for $300. You're going to get more duff for your money if you buy the quarter," he suggested.

The office door opened and Anna entered.

"Go out and get a quarter for me," he said to her.

Without saying a word she left, closing the door behind her. I was feeling pretty good. I had earned his trust by playing a backward, country boy hoping to learn something from a big city businessman. The Godfather seemed comfortable with our conversation. He went on, sharing various details with me about how his business was organized and the day-to-day operations of his drug empire.

I had gone from just hoping to get an introduction to a member of his organization to being offered a quarter ounce of crack by the Godfather himself. While he was talking, Anna walked back into the office.

She handed him a plastic bag that contained crack, then left the room without saying anything. The Godfather was much more receptive than Anna was; she came across as cold and distant.

The Godfather instructed Al to get his "meat" scale from the closet and hand it to him. "It's the most reliable scale you can get," he said.

He removed the crack from the plastic bag and placed it on the scale. "Looks like this one is a little heavy," he pointed out. "I'll still sell it to you for $300." He then spent some time explaining to me how to properly weigh the drugs.

Al asked the Godfather if we could come back the next day and watch how he cooked cocaine. "I usually start cooking around 9 a.m. if you want to stop in," he replied. "I'll show you the best way to cook it 'cause there's several ways to do it."

Taking a chance, I asked him how much he cooked up in a day. He replied, "I don't use duff. But if you were to give me a blood test, it would show me loaded with the shit. That's how much I cook." He went on to say that he probably cooked several ounces of crack a day, seven days a week. "When you make the best duff, you don't have any problem getting rid of it," he said.

I took $300 from my jacket and handed it to him. In return, he handed me the bag of crack. I had been in the house a long time when measured against the standards of a typical undercover drug buy.

But with the quarter ounce of crack and the incriminating statements the Godfather had made, the extra time was justified. I hid the crack inside my black leather biker coat and stood up. I told Al that we needed to get going.

Al reminded the Godfather that we would be back around 9 o'clock the next morning. Then we walked out of the office, down the hallway, and through the kitchen. The people standing around inside and outside of the house didn't have the same intimidating effect on me as they did when we had arrived. I didn't sense any danger or threat after meeting with the Godfather in his office.

As we walked to the car, I could see Yvonne resting her head against the backseat. I told Al that I didn't want Yvonne to know that we were able to buy drugs from the Godfather. I didn't want to take a chance that she would ask us to fire up a pipe and smoke some. Al agreed.

As we got into the car, Yvonne opened her eyes and sat up. She asked, "Well, how did it go?"

Al replied, "He didn't have anything."

I added, "I can't believe I drove all the way up here, sat in the kitchen for twenty-five minutes waiting for him to return, spent another half-hour talking with him, and left empty-handed."

Yvonne was very quiet as we drove back to her house. It seemed almost too quiet in the car. I still wondered why Yvonne had done an about-face and refused to go into the Godfather's house. I wasn't going to let her sudden mood swing spoil my victory, however.

After we dropped Yvonne off at her house, I told the surveillance team to meet us behind an empty building on Maury Street. As soon as I relayed the message, I shut off the recorder and the bug. I shouted, "Great job Al. We're in!"

"You better believe we're in, honey," Al responded with a big smile.

She asked me if I'd noticed who was armed. I told her that the only gun that I had seen was the rifle in the gun bag. "You're going to have to look for those things," she said, and began listing off all those who'd been armed.

She said that the first guy she hugged was Raymond Longstaff; he had had a handgun stuck in his waistband in the middle of his back. "The tall, skinny, Black guy that was over by the camper was Dwight Morrill," she said. "The butt of a gun was exposed at his waist in the front of his pants. And did you see the small gun in the drawer that was partially open in the kitchen?"

"No," I replied.

"Then you probably didn't notice the guy in the camper with the shotgun pointed in our direction as we left?" Al said.

"I was trying not to look too inquisitive and make them suspicious of me," I explained.

The only surveillance team members that met us at the vacant building were the sergeant and Tracy. Tracy jumped out of the sergeant's car and got in with us. The sergeant said he was disappointed that we had spent a lot of time in the house and didn't have any drugs to show for it.

"What do you mean?" I said. "I got a quarter ounce of crack and a tape full of incriminating statements made by the Godfather.

"Oh, that's great!" he said. "But the bug wasn't working worth a shit," the sergeant said. "All we got was bits and pieces. When you walked out of the Godfather's house the bug was audible. After getting into your car, didn't you tell that Black girl that he didn't have anything?"

"Oh, I see why we're not on the same page," I said. "I was giving her misinformation so we didn't have to give her any drugs."

The sergeant said he would meet us back at the office. We headed back to Al's house. Tracy lit up a cigarette and said that the only reason the sergeant had allowed the deal to continue was because from what he heard when the signal was strong enough to hear, he thought I wasn't in any danger.

That didn't make me feel very comfortable. If the signal from the bug was that bad, they could have missed the danger signal if I'd used it. Tracy said they'd played back the tape made from the bug and it was mostly static. I sure hoped that the recorder that I was carrying was working okay. A tape recording of our conversation would be solid evidence for a jury to hear. It would be much better than any testimony I would give based on memory.

On the way to Al's house, I told her not to have any contact with the Godfather or anyone else from the house. I didn't want to take the chance that they might talk about me. I asked her to get some sleep, and said I would pick her up around 8:30 in the morning.

As she got out of the car, Al gave each of us a hug. "We did good today. But tomorrow, we will do even better," she said with a big smile.

On the way back to the office, I filled Tracy in on all that had happened. She said, "This is going to be a great case. I'm excited to be able to work on it with you."

I asked her how the surveillance had gone. Tracy said that Stuart was the closest one to the house. At about 11:20 a.m., he radioed that he saw Al and me arrive at the Godfather's house. After we had entered the house, Stuart reported that three men left the house from the back door and took up positions outside the house.

The first man walked to the southeast corner of the property near the street, the second man walked to the south end, and the third man walked to the southwest corner.

Stuart told the surveillance team that all three men appeared to be working on the cars that were parked around the property, but he thought that it was just a cover. He felt they were actually keeping an eye out for trouble.

Stuart noticed that once the Godfather returned, the lookouts reported to someone at the backdoor in five-minute intervals. Stuart told the surveillance team that the three men continued to operate in that manner until Al and I left the house at 12:24 p.m.

I told Tracy that if my math were correct, it meant that we had been in the house for about an hour. She smiled and said, "Actually, that would be one hour and four minutes. But, who's counting?"

"I'm sure it felt like a long time. But trust me, the Godfather is going down!" I replied.

When we got back to the office, I went straight to the sergeant's office to fill him in on what had happened. The main thing that I wanted to talk to him about was my interest in returning the next day to watch the Godfather cook up a batch of crack.

The sergeant listened to me while he ate his lunch. He gave me his approval to return to the Godfather's house the next day and asked me to keep him informed about my plans.

I hurried back to my office to see if the tape recording I had made while I was with the Godfather was understandable. I hit the rewind button. I knew that if the tape were clear, I would have solid evidence against the Godfather. If not, it could come down to my word against his.

When I pushed the start button, the voices on the tape were clearly audible. It was as if the conversation had been recorded in a studio. I was ecstatic. "Yea!" I yelled out. "Touchdown, baby." That tape was so clear that anyone listening to it would think that the conversation was taking place right then and there.

Tracy and I field-tested the drugs that I had purchased from the Godfather. I had no doubt that they would test positive for the presence of cocaine, and they did. Tracy filled out the lab request, and we drove to Field Headquarters to place the drugs in an evidence locker.

Stuart paged us and asked if we were available to help him with a drug buy. We stopped at Burger King and picked up some food to go. Helping Stuart with his investigation wouldn't give me much time to review the meeting that I had had with the Godfather. Despite my excitement, I realized that I would have to turn my attention to Stuart's case and focus on that for a while.

# Chapter 12

Later that afternoon, I received a page from Al. Tracy and I were still helping Stuart with his investigation. I called Al from the car on my cell phone. She was talking a mile a minute. She was obviously very excited. I had to interrupt her and remind her that she needed to be discrete because I was calling from my cell phone and someone using a scanner could be monitoring our conversation.

Al was street savvy. She did not have a problem getting her message across. Nothing that she said during our conversation would have given away anything about the investigation to someone who might be scanning the call on his or her police scanner.

Al said she had had a visit from Baggy-D and Wendy a couple of hours earlier. They told her about a large quantity of methamphetamine and cocaine that they had just received. Because they were unable to hook me up the previous day, they wanted me to visit them that day.

I asked Al if she could arrange a three-way call between Baggy-D, herself, and me. That way I could feel him out before setting up another meeting. I requested the call because of the many hours of work we had put in the day before with no drugs to show for it. I wanted to explain to Baggy-D that I wasn't looking forward to driving all the way back to Indianapolis again after the wasted efforts of the previous day. It would also give me time to finish helping Stuart with his case.

Al said that she would give it a shot and call me back.

About twenty minutes later, as we were finishing the surveillance on Stuart's case, Al paged me. Since I was only five minutes from the office, I decided to wait and return her call from there. Before I reached the parking lot, my pager went off again. *It must be important,* I thought.

When Al answered her phone, she explained that she had it all set up. All she had to do was call Baggy-D. I told Al to give me a minute so that I could arrange to have our conversation recorded. She was still very excited. She was confident that it was going to be a great day for our team.

After setting up the equipment, I told Al to call Baggy-D. The phone went silent momentarily. Then I could hear a phone ring. After just one ring, Baggy-D answered, "Hello."

"Hi, I got him on the phone," Al said.

"Hi, Baggy-D," I said.

"Hey Bud, how ya doing? Ah, ah, sorry things didn't go well for ya. Ah, ah, however, I do have everything straight and waiting. Right now! So, there wouldn't be any going for a ride or anything like that this time. It will be right here waiting for you. Does that sound good?"

"Yeah, do you have good stuff?" I asked him.

"Yeah. Yeah. I got everything straight for ya. The last day we had to go through the runaround. And this time it won't be that way for ya," he said.

"From the sounds of it, you might have a little bit there," I stated.

"Yeah. Yeah," Baggy-D said.

"I'm thinking, if you have some good stuff, I'd want to be sure to get your bottom dollar," I told him.

"Okay. What's the order? No. Okay, I got the blond. Okay. Now, the blond I'm talking about, she can be either a rough rider (crack cocaine) or she can go smooth (powdered cocaine). Now, the other blond, she's always smooth (powdered methamphetamine)," Baggy-D explained.

"Okay, I understand," I said.

"Now, I call her the true blond. Okay? Of course, she doesn't get as hard as the other one," Baggy-D said.

Baggy-D was attempting to make sure that I understood that what he was describing was meth.

"If you got quite a bit there, how much money do I need to bring to get your bottom dollar?" I asked.

"On the true blond, which makes you go real fast, how much do you, how much do you want?" asked Baggy-D.

"She said you had quite a bit, ya know? And if I can get a good price," I said, hesitating.

"Do you want her for the whole night?" he asked.

I had no idea what he meant by that. I was hoping that he would be more specific. So, I went along with him hoping that "all night" would mean a large quantity, like a pound. So, I told him, "Yeah. I want her all night."

"All right! You want her all night. Okay. Say, oh, say twelve hours an 'O'," Baggy-D said, meaning he would sell me an ounce of meth for $1,200.

"Okay," I said. "It's not real weak, is it?" I was asking him if the meth had been heavily mixed with another type of powder.

"Oh, no. She's not weak at all. She can go all night!" he said laughing. "She'll make you go real fast.

"And of course, I've got the other blond here, too. And, ah, ah, you want her both ways, right?" He wanted to know if I wanted some of the cocaine in rock form and some of it in powder form.

"Well, probably the hard because I haven't learned the other stuff yet," I said, making it clear that I didn't know how to take powder cocaine and convert it into rock cocaine.

"Okay, I'm going to show you on that," he said. "So on her, did you want her for half a night or a quarter of the night (half ounce or quarter ounce)?"

"What is she going to cost me?" I asked.

"That would be best to talk with you about when you got up here. The phone, ya know? Hey. The phone, ya know?" Baggy-D said, indicating he was hesitant to give a price over the phone. "I think we talked about it earlier."

"So, the rent is going to be the same as the other?" I asked.

"Yeah," he replied.

"Do you want me to go over and check it out?" Al interjected.

"No! No! You got Baggy-D's personal guarantee. It's all good," Baggy-D said, laughing. "I just did some, okay. It's all good. I've checked it out. You know? It's good enough to eat with a spoon! I went to the trouble to make sure I had it all here for you now. I hope you appreciate that."

"Okay, I do," I said.

He added, "And, there won't be anyone here, to ah, to ah, that one guy I understand kind of intimidated you – Batman."

"It's not a matter of intimidation as much as it is for me to understand what his interest is in all of this," I replied.

"Oh. Okay. Batman is my doorman. He watches my door. He's my security. To make sure nothing happens when we do things," he explained.

"Well, you know I had something with me yesterday. Right?" I asked. I was referring to my gun.

"Yeah, yeah, so did I. I always do. That's normal man," Baggy-D said.

"That's not to make a threat against you. It's just to say that I work hard for what I have and to make a statement that I'm going to go home with what's rightly mine," I said.

"Sure. Exactly. Me too, brother. I ah, ah, I don't expect any less out of ya. Everybody I know, ya know, what it is. These girls get out of line. Get out of line. And you're fucked!" Baggy-D said, indicating that when drug dealers got out of line, you could get robbed or even killed. "Before we go, I want to say good-bye to you, sir. And, what time can I expect to see you tonight? I want to get this thing going."

"I'll be getting my things together and I'll be heading directly up to your house," I told him. "I'll be seeing you later, Baggy-D. Or, is it Saggy-D?" I said laughing.

"It's Baggy-D," he said. "You got it?"

"Okay. I got it," I said, still laughing.

After hanging up with Al and Baggy-D, I went to the sergeant's office. I needed to get his permission to set up the meeting and the drug buy after our regular quitting time of 4:30 p.m. By the time I was able to complete the necessary paperwork, get the money out of the safe, load the surveillance equipment, and so on it would probably be 4 or 4:30 p.m.

After hearing about my plans, the sergeant gave us permission to work overtime. But he said he wanted the deal to go down at Baggy-D's house. He did not want us to be driving all over Indianapolis like we'd done the previous day.

Next, I met with Tracy and filled her in on the latest information. I asked her to talk with the other detectives to make sure that they could work late. I went back to my office and called Paula to let her know that I wasn't going to be home on time.

At about 4:30 p.m., we gathered in the briefing room for the pre-buy meeting. I explained to the sergeant, Joe, Tracy, David, and Stuart that I was going to meet with Baggy-D at his house at 2605 Olson. During the meeting with Baggy-D, I would attempt to buy meth and crack.

Tracy and I thought that it would be a good idea to cut Al out of the meeting. That would allow us to deal directly with Baggy-D and not have to use a mediator. I explained our theory to everyone and told them that I would be calling Baggy-D before I met with him to see if he would agree to it.

I asked Joe to park the surveillance van near Baggy-D's house before I got there. That way we could get some information about the people coming and going from the house. I didn't trust Baggy-D when he said that he would be alone. We could also see who was dropping off the drugs if, by some chance, he did not have them at the house already.

At about 6 p.m., Joe called the office from the surveillance van. He said that he saw a White man carrying a long rawhide gun case into Baggy-D's house. He said that the man parked an old blue car near the house. A short time later, he saw two other White men enter through the front door of the house. Joe couldn't see where they had come from. It might have been from a side street.

I called Baggy-D at around 7 p.m. I told him that Al was not feeling well and that she had gone to a neighborhood clinic. I asked him if he wanted to do the deal another day or did he want me to come alone.

He said to come on my own. "Just hurry up," he said.

I met with the surveillance team one more time. After going over the plan again, I checked the bug, and we were off.

At about 7:25 p.m., I arrived at Baggy-D's house. Before I got out of the car, Joe called and told me that two of the three men had left. He thought that the first man who had carried the gun into the house was still inside. I had $2,000 cash on me. I was a little nervous because I didn't know what to expect. I was sure that there were guns in the house. I prayed that they were there for protection and not to kill me.

I told the surveillance team that there was a blue Monte Carlo parked in the driveway. I read the license plate information to them. I was equipped with a bug, a microcassette recorder, and my 9mm, semi-automatic handgun – something that I hoped I would not need to use.

The front door opened just as I reached the top step leading up to the house. There were lights on in the living room. Baggy-D greeted me. As I turned to watch him shut the door, I noticed a shotgun leaning up against the corner of the living room. Baggy-D locked the dead bolt on the door.

The television was on and it was very loud. I didn't see anyone else around, but I noticed that all of the doors to the adjoining rooms were closed. That was different from the previous day, so I guessed that we were not alone.

I asked him if he had the drugs. He said that he did. It was hard to talk because the television was blaring. I told Baggy-D that I wanted a half an ounce of each. I told him that I wanted to take the samples to a friend's house to test them to see how good they were. If the drugs were good, I would come back and buy some more.

"Oh, no," he said. "I'm not going to let you walk out of here without paying for it first."

I told him that he had misunderstood me. I would pay for them first. Then, I asked him what he wanted for the two half ounces. I told him that if they were good, I would be back to buy a pound of each. His response to my request would tell me how much he could handle and what size of a player he was.

Baggy-D said, "I don't have anything that big."

I told him that Al had given me the impression over the phone that he was holding "a lot of shit." He said that there was a mix-up and that he only had an ounce of each.

I asked him if he would sell me the two half ounces for $1,000. He said that $1,000 was too low. The drug that he and Al were talking about selling for $1,000 was weed (marijuana). He said Al had asked him how much he wanted for a pound of weed and he had replied $1,000. Baggy-D laughed and said that he wished that he could buy powder cocaine for $1,000 an ounce himself. He said, "Remember on the phone, I told you how much I'd sell it to you for."

I told Baggy-D that I remembered. "But I hoped that if I wanted to buy larger quantities, you would sell it to me for a better price. We were talking about just a couple ounces at a time," I said.

"You bet," he replied. "We can lower the price if you want to buy quantity."

I told him that if I were happy with the samples, I would buy larger quantities later on. That way, I wouldn't have to come back to Indianapolis as often. "My money is good. And, it's not a problem for me to come up with it," I assured him.

"This stuff is pure. I tried a little bit today," he said. "This shit is so good; I sat here and watched it as it lost two grams since 4 o'clock this afternoon. You know good meth will evaporate and lose weight over time. You have to double bag it and keep it in an airtight container."

We walked into the kitchen. He reached up above the cupboards and grabbed a light blue plastic bowl. When he took the lid off, he said, "See what I mean?"

"Yeah, I can smell it," I told Baggy-D.

"So, how much do you want? A half of each?" he asked.

"Yeah. That will work," I replied.

"That's all?" he asked.

"For right now," I said. "Then I'll be back ..." Baggy-D interrupted me.

"I'd rather have you go for the whole thing on that," he insisted. "I got one and a half right here. And on the phone, you said you wanted one to last you all night. You remember. I explained to you the different amounts and prices. And you said that you understood!" He was starting to get irritated.

I told him that I didn't want to say too much over the phone, but that I had thought we were talking about a pound when he said it would last me all night.

"A whole night is an ounce, and half a night is a half ounce," he said. "In fact, the most I ever get rid of is a whole at a time."

"Well, that's where the mistake is. I thought Al told me that you could do a pound tonight; what you really can do is an ounce," I said.

"I don't like working in that big of quantities unless I know the person real well. My friends only buy an ounce at a time. But of course, they don't have the drive that you do," Baggy-D said. "How much do you want?"

"Can you do a pound each at $1,000 an ounce?" I asked.

"Not now. Do you know what kind of money you're talking about?" he asked. "$16,000 a piece!"

"That's right, I guess. I don't have that much with me right now," I said, "but I can get it."

"I won't be able to help you on the pound. I can't do a full pound but I can get you a quarter," he said.

"Okay. What are you going to charge me for that?" I asked.

"I don't know. I'll have to check with my man on that. But the price goes way down. It would probably be around $3,500 or so," Baggy-D said after figuring it up in his head.

"Yeah. That's a good price," I said.

"So, why were you intimidated by the guy sitting on the couch yesterday?" he asked me. "That was just my doorman. You're a fool not to have a doorman. Are you straight with that?"

"Yeah. Can you go ahead and weigh her up?" I said.

"Yeah. I'll have to try and find some scales," he said as he rummaged through the drawers and cupboards. He couldn't find a scale in the kitchen, so he went into a room just off the hallway.

"She was supposed to tell you I wanted a half of each. I didn't realize there would be this mix-up," I yelled. "That's why I don't like to have to use a go-between."

"Me either," he yelled back. "I can't find the fucking things! Can you call her and have her bring the scales over."

He must have turned the television off because I could suddenly hear the stereo blaring. I asked him if he meant for me to call Al and have her bring over some scales. I told him that I really didn't have the time to wait for her drive up from the south side.

"I'm sure my hand scales are around here some place," Baggy-D said. He continued to search the house and finally found his hand scales. But when he went to get a plastic bag, the box was empty. So, he began walking around the house looking for a plastic bag to put the meth in so that he could weigh it.

*What an unorganized person,* I thought, looking at my watch. I had been in the house for about twenty-five minutes; I should have been in and out in less than ten minutes.

While he was searching the house, the phone rang. He talked with someone named Wayne for a couple of minutes, then went back to looking for a plastic bag. From my end, it sounded like Wayne wanted to place an order.

Then Baggy-D started to talk about Wendy, saying she had a big mouth. "She better watch herself or she will be looking at twenty-five years to life for something that she messed up," he said. "I'm not going to do that. You know what I mean? I'll go dead before I do twenty-five years. You know what I mean?"

He finally gave up looking for a plastic bag and said he was going to put the drugs in a small plastic container and seal it up. This was a first for me – buying drugs in a plastic bowl. He told me to pull a container out of a lower cupboard, which I did. Then I couldn't find a lid. So Baggy-D joined the search. I was sure that the members of the surveillance team monitoring the conversation were all having a good laugh.

We couldn't find a lid anywhere. I suggested he use the butter dish. I was trying to think of something that would get the deal moving along. He didn't like that idea. Instead, he decided to use a baby food jar. Finally, he found a small plastic container with a lid. "Will these work?" he asked me. I said they would.

He started by measuring the meth. I asked him how much it was going to cost me. He said that, normally, he got $1,700 for an ounce. "But since you're looking at doing quantities with me down the road, I want to give you a good price. Why don't we go $800 on this one for a half? And, I'm going to talk to my man and we'll try to work out something on the other (the crack)."

I told him that I had $1,500 with me and that I would pay whatever was right for the cocaine.

He asked me if I ever used drugs. I told him, "Not anymore." I explained that, a couple of years earlier, my drug habit was getting out of hand and my wife had told me to stop or it would be over between us. I asked him if it was "ass-kicking stuff."

"Fucking amen!" he replied.

He asked me if everything was okay. "You're not in any heat now, are you?" he said. I told him that I had been arrested for drunk driving once, but that was it.

He said that most of those he sold drugs to tried them out in front of him.

"Here's a half," he said, handing me the baby food jar. "You will want to put it in the freezer when you get to where you are going because it will dehydrate. I mean, it will evaporate."

I told him that it looked like it had been "stepped on" (mixed with a cutting agent). "No, I can guarantee that," he said. "This is the white stuff, not the yellow meth. There's a difference in the way you make them. When you cut the white stuff, it turns brown or yellow. You take a razor blade and when the metal touches the meth, it turns yellow or brown. Try it sometime. That way you will know if it has been stepped on. It will have a color to it. If it's pure white like this, it hasn't been stepped on. Remember that."

Just then, there was a knock on the door. Baggy-D looked surprised. By his reaction, it appeared that he thought someone was waiting for me outside. He acted like he didn't know what to do. He looked back and forth at me, then at the door. The person continued to knock rather loudly.

"Are you alone?" he asked me.

"Yes," I said.

"You got a gun with you, don't you?" he said.

His hesitation was making me nervous. I remembered back to the day before when I had noticed that someone had recently forced open his front door. I wondered if that was why he had had Batman sitting on the couch. He might have been the victim of a drug robbery. That would explain why he was being so cautious.

He told me to follow him to the door, and he walked over to the shotgun in the living room. I decided not to follow him.

I had never been in a situation like that before. I pulled out my handgun and took cover in the kitchen. Before he opened the door, he yelled, "Who is it?" I couldn't hear a response.

Baggy-D unlocked the dead bolt and opened the door. A Black man in his thirties stepped into the living room. Baggy-D told the man that he had caught him at a bad time. They moved to an area in the living room where I couldn't see them. From my position in the kitchen, I could hear them talking but I couldn't make out what was being said.

Fearing for my safety, I yelled out, "Have him take off until we're done with business!"

I heard Baggy-D say, "My man would rather have you wait outside until he leaves. Why don't you come back in about five minutes or so?"

Baggy-D walked back into the kitchen and explained that the man was a friend of his and it was no big deal. He watched as I put my gun back into my waistband. "I can't tell all my customers not to come over to the house 'cause how would I make any money?" he said. "You know what I mean?"

He went back to work. He measured out the powder cocaine into the small plastic container. Then he asked me if I wanted to learn how to cook it up. I told him to wait until the next time because I hadn't planned on being there that long. I needed to get going.

"So, you don't want me to show you how to rock it up?" he asked.

"Yeah, but not right now," I said. "I got to get going."

Baggy-D continued to putter around the kitchen as if he hadn't heard me say that I was in a hurry. I looked at my watch. I had been in the house almost forty-five minutes. He finally had the cocaine weighed. "Looks like twenty-eight grams to me," I said.

The phone rang. Baggy-D asked me to answer it. A man on the other end asked if it was Baggy-D's house and if he had reached the call service. "What?" I said, "Is this a call service?" Baggy-D told me to hand him the phone.

He talked to the man for a while, then told him that he would have to call him back. He explained to me, "I got a call service going and they forward the phones to this number when they have to step out for a minute."

I handed Baggy-D $1,500 in cash and told him that I had to be leaving. He asked me if I was going to want anymore that night. I told him that it depended on how much he could get and what the price was going to be. I told him that if he could get a quarter pound of meth, I would be interested. Baggy-D said that he would have to make a call first and see what he could get.

I told him that at the next meeting, I wouldn't bring anybody with me and I didn't want anybody else in the house, just him and me.

He agreed, "Cool."

"I appreciate your cooperation with all of the interruptions and the problems of finding my scales and a bag," he said.

The phone rang again. After a short conversation, Baggy-D asked the caller to call him back.

He gave me his phone number and asked me to call him if I liked the drugs. I unlocked the dead bolt and opened the door. I told him that I would call him in about fifteen minutes.

After driving out of the neighborhood, I looked in my rear view mirror. I could see the sergeant turn onto Second Avenue from a side street. I slowed down, and he pulled up beside me. I rolled down my window. "What took you so fucking long?" he said. "You should have been out of there thirty minutes ago."

"It was the best I could do," I replied. "Believe me, it felt like it took two hours to finish the deal."

"For the rest of us sitting out here in our cars, it seemed to take you eight hours. You're going to have to pick up the pace the next time," he shouted, and sped away.

I shook my head. I knew that I wasn't the best undercover officer, but I thought that I had done a good job at Baggy-D's, considering all of the obstacles that I had to overcome.

When I got back to the office, I filled out a property sheet. Meanwhile, Tracy tested the drugs that I had purchased. She got a positive result on both tests. I didn't think that Baggy-D would rip me off. He wanted the money and he saw the potential for future business.

Joe handed me the tape recordings that he had made from the bug. He laughed and said he had thought that he was going to have to call a time-out so that he could run back to the office and get another case of tapes. I asked him how the sound was from the bug. He said that he could hear CNN and heavy metal music. "I could even hear your heart beating when the dude knocked on the door," he said.

"I didn't know what to think when Baggy-D asked me to follow him to the front door with my gun drawn. I couldn't figure out if he wanted me to protect him or if he wanted to flush me out of the kitchen so that the guy hiding in the next room could take me out," I said.

"I think you did a great job," Tracy said. "But, I did wonder if the buy was going to last all night."

"Thanks for not leaving me," I said.

Then I remembered I had to call Baggy-D back and let him know if I wanted to pick up the quarter pound.

"If you do, you'll be there all by yourself 'cause that would mean an all-nighter the way this deal just went," Joe said.

"I was going to blow him off somehow and try to do it another day," I said.

So I went out to my car and called Baggy-D from my cell phone to make it sound legitimate. As it turned out, he couldn't meet with me anyway because his man was busy and he wasn't able to get the drugs. I told him that I would be in touch and that I was very pleased with my purchase. I told him that the blond lady was a real "spinner."

I called Al and told her about my meeting with Baggy-D. She was happy that things had gone well, but she said she wished that she had been there. I pointed out that if it hadn't been for her assistance, the deal would not have taken place. Besides, she had introduced me to the Godfather, which was a much bigger feat than buying drugs from Baggy-D.

I had had enough excitement for one day. I didn't even want to think about what was planned for the next day. All I wanted was to get something to eat, to take a shower, and to climb into bed. However, I did have a great feeling about what I had accomplished that day, and I was very excited about the next day. But if I didn't put it out of my mind, I wouldn't get any sleep.

# Chapter 13

*What a day!* I thought as I drove home. In my early days as a detective, either one of the two undercover assignments that I had just participated in would have been a dream come true. Each was filled with adventure and excitement. But to have both of them happen in the same day was simply hard to believe. It was overwhelming.

I knew that I probably wouldn't get any sleep. I felt like I had truly arrived, that I was actually a top-notch undercover officer.

I was right about the sleep; I tossed and turned all night. There were so many different directions that my case could go. The possibilities seemed endless. I was about to become a member of one of the largest and most successful drug organizations in the state of Indiana. I tried to stop my mind from wandering. I kept checking the clock on my nightstand. Time was ticking away.

The last time I remembered looking at the clock was at 2:28 a.m. The next thing I knew, my alarm was going off. After dropping Nate and Joel off at day care, I headed to the office. It was March 30, 1995.

On the way, my pager vibrated. I looked at the digital readout. It was Al. I picked up my cell phone and called her.

"Are you awake?" Al asked. "I've been awake since 4:30 a.m." She sounded very excited.

"I didn't get much sleep," I said. "I've got an idea. I'll run it past you when I get to the office."

When I pulled into the parking lot, I saw the sergeant's car parked near the door. I went straight to his office and asked him if he wanted to discuss my upcoming meeting with the Godfather. He told me that there were several things that he wanted to change.

"First, Joe has to figure out a way to improve the reception on the repeater," the sergeant said. "We can't sit there and guess what is going on in the house. You had a good day yesterday, but you were lucky. Things could have gone the other way.

"Second, I'm going to ask Chief Lang to have a patrol officer join us for the pre-buy meeting. If things get out of hand, I would feel better having a patrol unit close in case we need to hit the house."

"They're both good ideas," I replied.

"And finally, you need to be in and out of there in less than thirty minutes," the sergeant said. "You took way too much time on both undercover buys yesterday."

The sergeant yelled out to Joe, "Take a look at the repeater and see if you can improve the sound. Yesterday, it sounded like shit. You're the expert around here on the surveillance equipment – fix it!"

I gave Joe my car keys and he hurried outside.

"Do you want me to call Chief Lang?" I asked.

"No, I'll take care of it," the sergeant said.

One by one the other members of the unit arrived. I asked Tracy to remind them that we were having a pre-buy meeting at 8 a.m., then I began filling out the buy sheet.

I would be driving the same car. The only thing that was changed from the previous day's buy sheet was that Al and I would be the only ones going to the Godfather's house. It would be less complicated than the two previous attempts when we had tried to elicit Wendy and Yvonne's help, as we'd had to use moving surveillance teams then.

I called Al and told her that I was going to pick her up around 8:30 a.m. She asked me what the plans were for our meeting with the Godfather. I explained what we needed to do, then asked her for her opinion.

"Sounds great to me," Al said.

Joe came to my office and asked me to follow him out to the parking lot. I looked at the equipment that was in my car. "I took a drill and drilled a hole in the bottom of your trunk," Joe said. "This should allow the signal from the repeater to exit your car better. Then, I shortened the antenna so I could stand it straight up. With both of these changes, we should be able to hear you much better."

"Thanks, Joe. You're the best," I said. "That will make both the sergeant and me feel much better."

As I walked back inside, the sergeant asked me if I was ready to start the pre-buy meeting. "All I have to do is get the money out and get the serial numbers copied," I said.

"Let Stuart do that after the meeting. He can bring you the money when we meet you at the staging area after you pick up Al," the sergeant said. "Let's get this thing going."

"All I have to do is make copies of the buy sheet," I said.

"Do you have the layout of the house drawn on the big board yet?" the sergeant asked.

"Not yet," I said.

"Tell Tracy to make the copies and you get started on the board work," the sergeant said.

A few minutes later, we had all gathered in the briefing room. Each of us had a bulletproof vest and a helmet. Several members had their shotguns loaded and ready to go. The tool that we used to break down doors was leaning against the pop machine. The sergeant had his MP5 with a silencer attached next to him. Joe entered the briefing room with a bulletproof shield.

I realized that all of these items were ready for use as a precaution. However, they reminded me just how serious and dangerous my meeting with the Godfather was going to be. For a moment, I couldn't breathe. I wasn't acting in a television series. This was real. Since my college days I had dreamed of leading a big-time undercover operation. My chance had finally come.

As I started the briefing, I noticed the serious expressions on everyone's faces. They were also aware of what we were about to undertake. There weren't any jokes, and there wasn't any goofing around. John, the patrol officer assigned to serve as our "marked" backup, was sitting very straight in his chair.

I briefed everyone about the entire plan. Then I explained the individual assignments. Finally, I briefed them about the location where we would gather following my meeting with the Godfather. The sergeant asked if there were any questions. He reminded the surveillance team to stay alert to the surroundings and to my conversations with the Godfather.

The sergeant repeated my verbal warning signal, Bear Lake. "If you give us the signal, we will be in the house before there is any danger," he said, trying to assure me.

If everything went as well as it had the day before, then all of the precautions that we were taking wouldn't be necessary. I had a feeling the sergeant wasn't as optimistic about my second meeting with the Godfather as I was. But why should he have been? He hadn't heard for himself how the Godfather had befriended me at our first meeting. All the sergeant had to go on was my account of the meeting.

As I was leaving, I told the sergeant that I would meet the surveillance team at Safe-Way. The grocery store's parking lot would serve as the staging area. Tracy followed me in her car as I drove down to pick up Al. Many thoughts were running through my mind.

None of them were bad or frightening. Instead, I thought about the Godfather taking large amounts of cocaine and walking me through the steps he used to make crack. I considered what we might talk about during the process. If I could, I wanted to steer the conversation toward his business operations. I planned to ask him about the amount of crack that he had made over the years, the amount of money that he had made through his illegal drug dealings, and the amount of money that he had made through prostitution and fencing stolen goods.

I could feel my heart beating faster. I was excited about the opportunity ahead of me. With Al's help, I would be opening up the biggest case in the department's history, a case that would catapult my career to the next level. I hoped that it would lead to my being promoted to the Drug Enforcement Administration (DEA) task force, which in my opinion was the ultimate assignment for a narcotics detective. It would mean I would work only on federal investigations. Vince, a Riverside County detective, had been a DEA task force member for several years. His investigations had taken him outside the state of Indiana, something I desired.

The next thing I knew, I was pulling into Al's driveway. I didn't have to get out of the car as Al was already out the front door and heading straight for the car. She was carrying a large plastic cup filled with her usual soda pop. Al was wearing a black biker's jacket, a blue sweatshirt, tight-fitting jeans, and black-and-white tennis shoes.

Her hair was filthy, but she had it neatly combed to the right. One of her plain-label cigarettes was hanging out of her mouth. She had a look of determination on her face. Behind her I saw a bulldog jump up against the porch door.

Al opened the passenger door and got in. She had on cheap perfume. Her clothes, however, still smelled like a combination of cigarette smoke and bulldogs. I couldn't help notice the bright red lipstick she was wearing.

"What a great day it is!" she said. "Are you ready to do some cooking?"

"I sure am," I said, smiling at her.

Tracy followed Al and me to the Safe-Way parking lot. Along the way, I told Al that our meeting today with the Godfather had to be less than thirty minutes. I also told her that I wanted to keep the conversation focused on the Godfather and his organization. I didn't want to talk about my background or me.

Al listened intently. I had become very comfortable working with Al on the undercover operation. In a sense, I felt like I was her student. I was playing the role of a criminal but she had actually lived the life, so I could learn a lot from her.

Our meeting in the Safe-Way parking lot was brief. The sergeant asked me to turn on the bug to measure the signal. It appeared to be working fine. The sergeant's last words to me were "be careful."

We were ready to go. I gave the sergeant the "thumbs-up," and we were off. The drive to 1000 S.E. Lexington was quiet. We were both gearing up for what was to come.

As we turned the corner, I could see several old cars parked in front of the Godfather's house. I noticed that there were some additional men serving as security and patrolling the property.

I turned on my microcassette recorder and hid it under my clothes.

Al said, "Remember, God is with us. There is nothing to fear."

"Yes, He is," I said.

I assumed my role as a farm boy from southern Indiana. Al and I got out of the car. As we walked toward the house, I noticed that no one was paying attention to us. After my conversation with the Godfather the previous day, maybe we weren't a threat to them.

One man ignored Al when she greeted him. No one stopped to question us. Al opened the back door, and we entered the porch. We climbed the steps leading up to the kitchen. When Al and I entered the kitchen, people scattered.

Suddenly, the room was silent. The light was very low. The smell of freshly brewed coffee came from the pot on the counter. And unlike the previous day, the kitchen wasn't cluttered with dirty dishes.

Anna was the only one left sitting at the kitchen table. She was dressed in jeans and a dark-colored sweatshirt. Next to her, there was a full ashtray. Several cigarettes were still smoldering. She was holding onto a cup of coffee with both hands. Her head was hanging down.

"Hi, Anna," Al said. "I see you're up and dressed."

"Yep," Anna replied. There was silence again.

Al tried to start up a conversation but Anna did not seem eager to join in.

I could hear movement upstairs and in the living room. Then I heard the back door open and close. No one entered the kitchen, however. Whomever it was must have stayed on the back porch.

The atmosphere was very different than it had been the previous day. I looked at Al with concern. I could sense that she was feeling a little uneasy and I knew I was.

The Godfather entered the kitchen and sat down. He was as distant and cold as Anna was.

"Good morning, Robert," Al said.

"Morning," he said softly. He looked down at the kitchen table and avoided making eye contact with us. He took a sip from a coffee cup and set it back down on the table.

A blanket of silence again fell over the house. I couldn't hear anyone moving anywhere in the house. Again, Al attempted to start up a conversation. Each time she tried, the responses from the Godfather and Anna were minimal. What had happened?

Maybe I was overreacting. Maybe Anna and the Godfather had had an argument before we arrived. And if something was wrong, someone would have called Al and told her not to come. We definitely wouldn't have been able to enter the house if the plans had changed.

After several minutes of silence, Al finally said, "What's the matter, Robert? You seem to have something on your mind. Is there anything I can do to help?"

Silence. I looked at the Godfather. He sat in his chair still looking down at his coffee cup. Anna sat motionless and without expression. She was also looking down at the table. More silence.

"What's the matter, Robert?" Al said again.

Still more silence.

It was a far cry from listening to the Godfather as he explained how I should transport drugs; how much he sold eights, quarters, and other quantities of drugs for; and what kind of scale he used to weigh the drugs. I could only hope that the bug was working. If something did go wrong, the surveillance team needed to hear me give the verbal danger signal.

I waited for the Godfather to say something, anything that would indicate why we were receiving the silent treatment.

Slowly, he looked up from the table. He looked first at Al, then at me. His was obviously upset. In his deep voice he said, "Yvonne said that when you two were over here yesterday, she could hear everything that was being said in the house while she was sitting in the car. She said you guys were wired and he was a cop!"

Again, he looked at Al, then at me. Anna looked up from the table and made eye contact with me. Her eyes were as cold as ice. The Godfather had been slumped over in his chair, but he had suddenly straightened up.

The silence in the house was momentarily broken by the sound of footsteps. I did not see anyone, but the footsteps confirmed my earlier suspicions that someone was hiding in the living room.

I could feel my heart pounding against my chest. A shiver raced up my spine. My palms were sweating.

I wasn't prepared for a confrontation. I was caught completely off guard.

I wondered how Al was going to respond.

My instincts kicked in and I went to work. I became the farm boy from southern Indiana. I had no choice; either I convinced the Godfather that I was not a cop, or I would become one of his victims.

135

I looked him straight in the eye and said, "That's bullshit! She's just mad because we wouldn't give her any crack when we left yesterday!"

"Yea," Al said. "He's my friend. He ain't no cop."

"I don't want any trouble with you," I reassured him. "If things aren't cool, we'll just leave 'cause I don't want any trouble here."

I opened my leather biker's jacket and lifted up my shirt to expose my upper body. I prayed that, by taking the initiative to show him that I wasn't wearing a wire, I wouldn't be searched. How would I have explained the microcassette recorder I had hidden on me? The bug that I was using was disguised as a pen. I knew that he probably wouldn't ever find it.

I never even considered unzipping my coat pocket and removing my small five-shot, .380 caliber Walther PPK semiautomatic. I realized that if I exposed my gun, it wouldn't help me get out safely. It would have been seen as a threat. I probably would have had to use it. I might have ended up needing to shoot my way out of the house.

I didn't have enough ammunition to do that. Besides, Al had warned me that the Godfather and Anna both carried handguns when they were doing business. If I had made a move to unzip my coat pocket and remove my gun, I could have been shot by either one of them. With someone hiding in the living room, lookouts positioned upstairs, and armed security guards outside, I wouldn't have had a chance of getting out by using my gun.

My only chance of staying alive was to bluff my way out. I needed Al to remain calm and not fall apart.

Suddenly, Al got up from her chair and opened up her coat. Then, she lifted up her top to show the Godfather and Anna that she wasn't wired either. "Robert, I've known you for fifteen years. I wouldn't bring no cop in here on you!" Al said.

My thoughts turned to the repeater. Was the signal strong and clear? Were the sergeant and the surveillance team aware of the threat that I was facing?

If the signal was spotty like it was the previous day, would the sergeant recognize my predicament? Was he concerned that he might miss me giving the verbal danger signal? Knowing that safety came first, would the sergeant order the surveillance team to attack and enter the house in order to protect me?

From my previous surveillance experience and the information that Al had given me, I realized that the sergeant could not approach the house without being spotted by the Godfather's security force. If the sergeant gave the order to attack and enter the house, there would be verbal warnings passed along to the Godfather from his security guards. Neither Al nor I would stand a chance of getting out of the house unharmed.

The Godfather calmly reached for the phone that was sitting on the kitchen table. He picked up the receiver and punched out a number. Anna continued to glare at me as she sat motionless in her chair.

Who was he calling after making such a serious accusation? There was silence while he finished dialing. The phone was ringing on the other end.

"Is Yvonne there?" he asked. He was calling Yvonne Jametta. "Yea, Yvonne, yesterday when Al and her friend were here, what was it that you said you could hear us talking about?"

The Godfather stared at me. There was silence in the room. At that moment, I realized that I was in trouble. If the speaker volume on the repeater had been jarred during the bumpy ride to the Godfather's house, Yvonne could have heard everything that was being said while we were driving. The volume could have been low enough that only she could hear our conversation coming from the repeater in the trunk, since the speaker on the repeater was less than a foot away from where she was sitting.

That would explain why she had suddenly become quiet as we approached the house and why she had decided not to take us inside.

"Yeah. Yeah. What else?" he asked.

I could envision how it was going to play out. My only hope was that the sergeant would not give the order to attack and enter the house. If he did, I was convinced that there would be a lot of gunfire that might result in many injuries and, maybe, even death. At that moment, the Godfather was in control. Our fate was in his hands.

The conversation between the Godfather and Yvonne went on and on. It seemed like Yvonne was doing most of the talking. What was she telling him?

My heart was pounding. Time seemed to be standing still. If I ever needed God, it was then! I could not believe what was happening. It was like having a nightmare. I was shaking. If I was having a bad dream, I wanted it to end. Unfortunately, it wasn't a dream.

The room remained silent while the Godfather listened to Yvonne's version of the previous day's events. Suddenly, Al blurted out, "Ask her if she heard us talking about painting the kitchen pink."

I wondered what Al was doing. We hadn't talked about painting the kitchen pink. Or, had there been a conversation about the kitchen that I had simply forgotten? What an odd thing to suggest to the Godfather.

Then, it came to me. Al was trying to set a trap for Yvonne in order to discredit her.

"Did you hear us talking about painting the kitchen pink?" the Godfather asked.

Again, there was silence while he listened to Yvonne. The Godfather looked away from us. Then, he looked at me. Finally, he glanced over at Al.

"Yeah. Yeah. Then what?" he asked. He looked at me with a cold, deadly look. "I want you to repeat what you just said."

He looked at me and took the phone away from his ear. He told me to take the phone and listen to what Yvonne was saying. The whole time, he maintained direct eye contact with me. I had never had someone look at me the way that he did. His cold stare was very intimidating and very frightening.

I got up from my chair, reached for the phone, and put it to my ear. I tried to act confident. But, I wondered, what was my body language saying about how I was feeling? I was scared. No. I was terrified.

I couldn't believe that Yvonne might be giving a word-for-word account of what had been said the previous day. How was I going to respond after hearing Yvonne tell her version of what had happened?

I thought that the game was up. At that point, I had absolutely no hope of getting out of the house unharmed. Because of the speaker on the repeater broadcasting our conversation, Al, the surveillance team, and I were facing real danger. I had longed to work on a big case, but I felt as though my selfish desires had landed us all in the middle of what was clearly becoming a no-win situation. Working undercover wasn't fun anymore.

It had come down to me having to listen to my own words being repeated back to me. What kind of a mind game was the Godfather playing? It looked like he was enjoying himself.

As I put the phone to my ear I could hear Yvonne say, "I heard the door open and close. Then, Som asked you how he could get the truck started. And then, there was some more static coming from that thing."

I rolled my eyes to show the Godfather that I wasn't impressed by what she was saying. I took the phone away from my ear and shook my head as if I couldn't believe what Yvonne was claiming to have heard. I handed the phone back to the Godfather. I was trying to convince him that the statements that Yvonne was making didn't threaten me.

For the first time, I could see a ray of hope. Because of our initial reaction to his accusation and because of the sketchy nature of Yvonne's information, I wondered if there could be some doubt in the Godfather's mind about my being a cop. Was it going to be enough to get us out of the house unharmed?

Then the Godfather yelled into the phone, "Why didn't you report this to one of us immediately, when you thought he was a cop and there I sat in the house with some kind of a law enforcement investigation going on? Why would you just sit there in the car and let this guy gather evidence against my organization and me? You should have gotten out of the car and stopped it from continuing! There were all kinds of people you could have told. They could have gotten the information to me!"

It sounded as though the Godfather was scolding Yvonne. I could sense that the dark cloud hanging over us was beginning to lift.

"Don't you know that by you claiming he was a cop, someone could get a jacket? That kind of statement could get somebody killed!" he said.

I looked at Al. She had a look of anger on her face. She shook her head in disbelief. She was doing a great job of acting.

Anna was fidgeting in her chair. Her stern look and the Godfather's cold stare were unsettling.

But as the focus of the conversation between the Godfather and Yvonne shifted in our favor, Anna began to relax.

The room was silent as the Godfather listened to Yvonne's apologies.

"Okay. Okay. You just stay there at the house and I'll talk to you in a little while. Just remember that the next time, yeah. Well this is a very, very serious thing you have done!" he said, then he hung up the phone.

I waited for his next move. I thought that the danger had passed. There was silence while he collected his thoughts. He looked over at Anna, who was sitting quietly.

I glanced at Al. I wondered what she was thinking. Her expression was the same as it had been when we first sat down at the table. Yvonne's statements did not seem to affect her. Al was using her body language to make it very clear that she had done nothing wrong. She had a very confident look about her. She sat tall in the chair and leaned forward.

The Godfather looked at me, then at Al. "When a friend of mine makes an accusation against someone as she did, I had to follow it up for my own protection," he said. "I can't have a cop working in my organization. That could take me down the river for a long, long time. You understand, don't you? I just can't let something as serious as this go unchecked."

"I understand your position," I said. "But I'm not very happy with Yvonne. I wouldn't come in here knowing what Al had told me about you and start any trouble. That would be crazy!"

I removed my dark glasses so that he could see my eyes. "I'm not a cop," I said. "And something better be done about this woman that I don't even know who is spreading such rumors. She's your friend. So if you want to take care of it, that's cool. But if you want to leave it up to me, I'll make sure she knows how I feel about the situation she put me in!"

"I'll take care of it," he said.

I knew that in my role as a drug dealer, I had to make threats of violence. I still was not out of the house safely and I had to continue playing my part. If I didn't, I would have been seen as either weak or afraid. At that point, I would have said anything to simply get out of the Godfather's house alive.

"We had to make sure you weren't a cop," Anna said, appearing more relaxed and calm.

Al looked at me and asked, "What do you want to do now?"

Without waiting for me to answer, she looked at the Godfather and Anna. "Are things cool now?" she said. "Can we go on with business?"

"Things are cool," Anna said. "We just had to take care of this first."

"There's no problem now," the Godfather said. "We can get started if you would like."

I knew that we had just avoided a potentially serious situation. The sergeant and the surveillance team would be more than happy to just call it a day. To continue with the drug deal would be more than any of us could manage. It would be enough of an accomplishment for one day if I left the house safely and no one was harmed.

"I don't know about today. It's not everyday I come to Indianapolis and go through something like this," I said hesitantly. "If it's okay, I think I'll go back home and we'll try this another day."

"It's up to you," the Godfather said. "I can show you the method I use today or, if you feel like coming back some other time, that's fine, too."

"I'm pretty hot right now about Yvonne and probably won't be thinking very clearly until I calm down. It would probably be better if we come back another time," I said, standing up.

Al followed my lead and pushed her chair away from the table. As she stood up, she reassured Anna and the Godfather that she would never hurt them.

While Al was talking, I went to the porch. There was a large bearded man standing in front of the main entrance to the house. It was the only way out and the door was barricaded shut with a large two-by-four section of wood. We were locked in.

If the sergeant and the surveillance team had tried to enter the house, they would have had a very difficult time trying to get the door open. While they were working on getting into the house, the security force guarding the Godfather and the property would have had ample time to get in position and start shooting. And, if that had been the case, then Al and I would have definitely been shot by the Godfather and Anna. The surveillance team members could have been severely wounded as well.

The guard at the door was waiting for the Godfather to give him the signal to remove the two-by-four and open the door for Al and me.

"Are you ready, Al?" I said, interrupting her conversation.

I told the Godfather I would see him again soon. The Godfather nodded to the doorman, and the doorman removed the board.

I waited for Al to reach the porch. I turned and waved good-bye to Anna and the Godfather. Then, we walked out of the house.

Al and I walked in silence to the car. I was concentrating on getting to the car and getting away from danger. The car was parked about seventy-five feet away, but it felt like a mile.

Al and I reached the car and got inside. I started the engine and backed out of the Godfather's yard.

As I drove off, Al reached for my hand. She squeezed tightly. "Thank you, God. We did it!" she said.

She had been superb. If Al had shown any hesitation in her support for me, I was convinced that things would have ended much differently. She had saved not only my life but also the lives of my fellow officers.

"I told you that God would be with us today," Al said.

"He sure was!" I said.

As I shifted into drive, I said out loud, "We're okay. We're leaving westbound on Lexington. We will meet you behind McDonald's on S.E. 14th Street." I was talking to the sergeant and the surveillance team. I did not know if the bug was working or if they were even aware of the danger we had just encountered.

# Chapter 14

About three blocks from the house, I saw Stuart pull out from a side street and pull in behind us. He followed us as we drove south on S.E. 14th Street. I kept an eye on my rearview mirror in case the Godfather had ordered someone to follow us.

Minutes later, my cell phone rang. "Are you okay?" the sergeant asked.

"Sure. We're fine," I replied.

"I had a couple of cars stay in the area and watch for any counter surveillance as you left his house. They just called me and said they didn't see anyone leave the house after you did," the sergeant said. "I'll meet you back at the office."

As we pulled into the McDonald's parking lot, Al asked me what we were going to do about Yvonne. She offered a few suggestions, all of which were out of the question because of the oath that I had taken to serve and protect.

Tracy got into the car and rode with us to Al's house. Along the way, I asked Al not to speak with any of the Godfather's people, including Yvonne, until I had a chance to talk with the sergeant about the case. It would be natural for Al to want to settle a score for the position in which Yvonne had put us and that would have just made a bad situation worse.

Al asked me if she could smoke a cigarette. "Sure," I said. "The way you didn't fold under the pressure, you can light up two cigarettes!"

"I think I will have one, too," Tracy said.

We pulled into Al's driveway. "It sure is nice to be back home," Al said. Then she reached over and gave me a big hug. I knew I owed her a lot. She had given a great performance. Without her convincing act, I knew that we wouldn't be sitting in her driveway at that moment.

I thought about the first time that I had talked with Al on the phone. It had been the night of Nate's Fun Night at school. She had told me that she would do anything in her power to help facilitate the Godfather's arrest and take his organization down.

She had decided to risk everything to get the job done. Fortunately for us, it hadn't come to that.

After holding on to me for a couple of seconds, Al asked if she could give me a kiss on the cheek. "You did as much as I did to give us the opportunity to walk out of his house alive," she said. "When you took off your glasses and let him see your eyes while proclaiming you weren't a cop, that was excellent!"

I didn't say anything. I just turned my head and leaned toward her. She gave me a quick kiss. I told her to keep a low profile until I got back to her. Al opened the car door and got out. She waved good-bye as we pulled out of the driveway.

As we drove back to the office, my thoughts were quite different than they had been the previous day. The day before, I had had the feeling that I was invincible. I had thought I was a rising star. I had thought of so many possibilities and so many angles from which I could infiltrate the Godfather's organization.

Suddenly, I no longer had any dreams of the future. I was consumed by what had gone wrong. I had been so close to reaching my goal. And then in less than twenty minutes, everything had changed.

The drive back to the office went by quickly. When I pulled into the lot I noticed that the surveillance team members were already back. I parked my car, grabbed the repeater from the trunk, and walked inside. The office was quiet. Nobody was out and about. It was like a ghost town.

After putting the equipment away, I stopped by the sergeant's office. He was sitting there with the lights off. The only light in the room came through the window that faced the parking lot. And because the sky was overcast, there wasn't much light in his office at all.

The sergeant was sitting behind his desk staring out the window with a blank look on his face. I noticed his stereo was off and an unopened can of Pepsi was on his desk.

I sat down on the couch. "Sorry things got so messed up today," I said. "Things didn't turn out like I had hoped."

"Oh?" the sergeant said with a puzzled look on his face. "I think things went okay. You walked out of the house, didn't you?"

Then it hit me: I was lucky to be alive. I could feel my pulse quicken and my palms start to sweat. A lump was growing in my throat.

"Yeah, I guess things did go okay today," I said.

My eyes filled with tears. The lump in my throat had grown so large that I wasn't able to speak. I stood up and walked out of the sergeant's office. I continued walking until I got to my car, thoughts of fear racing through my mind. I opened the car door and climbed inside. The confrontation that I had had with the Godfather suddenly hit me like a ton of bricks. I put my hands on my face and began crying uncontrollably.

I realized then that I had been living in my own little fantasy world. The games that I had been playing with drug dealers were not games at all. I was not an actor in a television drama. I was not an actor in a suspense movie. Everything around me was real. And today my dream of being an undercover officer had brought me face-to-face with death.

I continued to sob. A deep sense of anguish came over me. I had two children that I loved more than anything. I had a wife, a mother, a father, a brother, and a sister. Because of my job and the choices that I had made, I had nearly lost my life and my family had nearly lost me.

God must have been watching over me. My experience, however, was a wake-up call for me.

After calming down and waiting for my eyes to clear up, I walked back into the building and into the sergeant's office.

"I know that the Godfather said I could come back another day, but I'm done working undercover. I'm not going back into that house!" I declared.

"That's okay with me," the sergeant said. "It's your call, but I'd have to agree with you."

The sergeant reached for the phone. Over the intercom he announced, "Meeting in my office. Now."

The mood was somber as the members of the unit arrived and quickly sat down. When everybody was there, the sergeant said that he wanted to talk about my meeting with the Godfather.

"Joe, you did an excellent job of making the necessary adjustments on the repeater. It sounded as if I were right there in the room with Steve!" the sergeant said. "I would hate to even think what would have gone down this morning if the sound had not been so clear."

He looked around the room at all of us. "You all did a great job sitting tight and waiting for my instructions," he said. "You kept the radio traffic down and did not panic.

"Steve, we were ready to come in and get you out of there if you had given the danger signal," the sergeant said, "But, you did your job and remained calm.

"Steve told me prior to this meeting that he is not going back to the Godfather's house. He and I will talk it over and decide what to do next," he said. "That's it. Get some work done."

I went to my office and I rewound the tape recording from my meeting with the Godfather. The sound was crystal clear. Listening to it sent shivers up my spine. As I heard the words again, I could see the Godfather's face. All of the emotions that I had felt earlier came rushing back.

I could not get the fear out of my mind. My senses seemed to be in overdrive. I could still smell the Godfather's kitchen, hear Yvonne's voice as she talked about the previous day, see the large man standing in front of the barricaded door, and smell Anna's perfume.

I felt vulnerable and a fear of death overwhelmed me. My thoughts about the investigation were replaced with an endless replay of my near-fatal meeting with the Godfather.

In an attempt to get the memories of that horrifying experience out of my mind, I decided to dictate my report. After several attempts, I stopped. I couldn't concentrate.

Over the intercom, I heard the sergeant call me to his office. On my way there, I fought back tears. Thankfully, the hallways were empty. Actually, it was almost eerie. There were no radios blaring, and no one appeared to be working on their cases. They were all sitting in their offices. I assumed they were thinking about what might have happened if things had gone differently.

"I just got off the phone with Brent Turner (an FBI special agent)," the sergeant informed me. "I told him about your run in with the Godfather this morning. I asked him if he would take the case and the Godfather federal."

"Yeah?" I said.

"He told me that with the crack buy you did with the Godfather yesterday and with the guns that were involved, he estimated that at a minimum, the Godfather would be looking at fifteen years to life!" the sergeant said with a big smile.

"Thanks. That's great news!" I said.

"You will need to meet with him and fill him in on what you have. Then Turner and you can set up a meeting with the attorney general's people to see how they want to proceed," the sergeant said.

That bit of information was enough to take the edge off. It comforted me to know that the sergeant had taken the initiative to call and make sure that the federal authorities were going to pick up the case. If the Godfather was charged under the state code of Indiana, he could only receive a ten-year maximum sentence. The reality of a state charge was that the Godfather would probably be released from prison in less than three years.

I went back to my office and tried to work on my report. I skipped lunch. I didn't have much of an appetite. The rest of the afternoon went by quickly. The other members of the unit seemed to distance themselves from me, not realizing that I could have used their support.

When I got home that evening, I told Paula about my meeting with the Godfather. I intended to minimize the danger that I had faced so as not to alarm her. We had only been married a little over a year and I thought it would be best to keep it from her.

But as I started to tell her what had happened, I had flashbacks of being in the house with the Godfather. Instead of telling her an abbreviated version, I found myself describing every little detail. But to my surprise, she didn't react the way I expected her to.

She wasn't in the least bit moved by the events that I was sharing with her. It was as if I was telling her a fish story. But, it wasn't a fish story. I wasn't making more of it than it had been. I thought she would be stunned or even frightened. Instead, she was indifferent. She didn't reach out to hold my hand or give me a hug. When I finished telling her about all that had happened, she simply said, "You sure can lie convincingly."

It was a slap in the face. I could have been killed and she was focusing on what I had said to the Godfather in order to get out of the house alive. But I knew why she had said it. Our relationship was based on lies. It all started when we met, and periodically, she would lash out at me because of her insecurities and misgivings about our relationship.

I had met Paula and her sisters in a hotel lounge in Chicago, Illinois, on October 9, 1993. I was there with several of my friends attending a Bears football game during a weekend away from our wives.

They were there celebrating the fortieth birthday of one of her sisters. Even though Paula and I were married to other people, we started a relationship that weekend. Then I went home to my wife in Indianapolis and she went home to her husband in a Chicago suburb. We maintained a long-distance relationship for quite some time.

During one of our secret phone calls, I remember telling her that if she weren't a Christian, I would not even consider making a commitment to being in a relationship with her. I justified my decision to commit adultery by convincing myself that it was okay because I was entering a loving Christian relationship.

We were able to arrange several romantic liaisons. Of course, we had to lie to our spouses to pull them off. At the time, it seemed okay because we both thought that our marriages were broken and beyond repair. Up until my relationship with Paula, I had never lied to my first wife. Suddenly, I found it easy. It was as if I were lying to a drug dealer in an undercover role. I was doing at home what I did everyday at work. It didn't bother me. I didn't feel the least bit guilty. Eventually the truth came out, and Paula and I got divorces. Then we got married.

So from the beginning, Paula and I did not have trust. We had a relationship based on deceit and sin, not on Christian love. Even after getting married, it was apparent we hadn't built a foundation of trust.

The retelling of my encounter with the Godfather that day was clearly a reminder to her of how skilled I was at lying. And it scared her to think that I could be so convincing.

# Chapter 15

In August 1995, the FBI and the Riverside County Sheriff's Office raided the Godfather's house at 1000 S.E. Lexington Street. Two truckloads of stolen property were confiscated. Handguns, long-barreled guns, ammunition, cash, scales, and drug paraphernalia were also seized as evidence.

Within a month, the case was brought before a federal grand jury, which handed down a thirteen-count indictment charging eight people with committing crimes as part of their involvement in a large drug operation.

Seven of the eight people charged in the case pleaded guilty to various federal drug violations. Robert Porter, a.k.a. the Godfather, pleaded not guilty.

On April 1, 1996, at 8:00 a.m., the Godfather's jury trial in United States District Court in the Northern District of Indiana before The Honorable Charles R. Wolff, Chief Judge, began.

He was charged with using his junk business as a cover to sell stolen goods that he had acquired during drug deals. He was also charged with preparing and delivering crack, methamphetamine, and cocaine to people in and around Indianapolis. And, he was charged with supervising the collection of the money owed for the drug deals.

During the trial, testimony revealed that the drug operation had started in early 1994 and had ceased to exist when the Godfather was arrested on August 16, 1995.

Testimony also showed that the Godfather's security system included a closed-circuit television camera, which was located in his office, several night-vision scopes, and a couple of police scanners. The Godfather used pagers to communicate with his drug customers. His customers had used pagers to contact other buyers in their efforts to sell the drugs for profit.

Marcus Morrill testified that he had introduced the Godfather to crack in April 1994. Since that time, Marcus said that he had served as a junior partner in the business. He had helped organize the security, had distributed drugs, and had carried a gun as protection.

Marcus also testified that since 1994, the operation had produced and sold approximately five to ten kilograms of crack, about the same amount of powder cocaine, and about ten kilograms of methamphetamine.

Anna Streeter testified that she had learned about the Godfather's involvement with drugs sometime in 1992. She was seventeen years old at the time and was employed as a dancer at a strip joint located south of the Indianapolis city limits. She had quit her job and had moved in with the Godfather.

Anna said in November 1994 she began handling duties such as weighing the drugs, getting the drugs from the garage for distribution, and hiding the money in the garage. She also testified that she had accompanied the Godfather on various trips to obtain large quantities of cocaine and methamphetamine. At the Godfather's insistence, she had carried a .380 caliber, semiautomatic handgun.

Anna estimated that since 1994, the operation had produced and sold approximately seventeen kilograms of crack, about the same amount of cocaine powder, and a large quantity of methamphetamine. Her estimates were different from Marcus Morrill's because she had weighed the drugs and he didn't.

Various customers testified against the Godfather. Greg Black said he had purchased at least ten pounds of methamphetamine from the Godfather between March 1995 and July 1995. Dante Butters, a.k.a. Baggy-D, and Raymond Longstaff said they had purchased various amounts of crack, cocaine, and methamphetamine from the Godfather during 1994 and 1995.

Both Baggy-D and Longstaff verified the sequence of events that had taken place on March 29, 1995. Longstaff testified that he delivered drugs to Baggy-D and hid in one of the bedrooms on the day I purchased half an ounce of methamphetamine and half an ounce of cocaine at Baggy-D's house. Longstaff said he purchased the drugs he delivered to Baggy-D from the Godfather.

To show the jury how violent the Godfather was, the prosecutor asked Baggy-D to testify about an occasion when the Godfather had confronted him about a drug deal of Baggy-D's that had taken place in Fort Williams, Indiana, in which Baggy-D had lost money selling the Godfather's drugs. Baggy-D had insisted that he had been ripped off.

Baggy-D said that the Godfather had vowed "to make it right," and had asked Baggy-D to go to Fort Williams with him to get the money. He had warned Baggy-D that he should be prepared to shoot people if necessary. Baggy-D testified that he had not accompanied the Godfather on his trip to resolve the matter.

Other witnesses testified that they had traded property for drugs with the Godfather. Many of the witnesses admitted that most of the property was stolen goods. A number of witnesses also testified that on a monthly basis, the stolen property was moved by van or truck from the Godfather's house to another location in Indianapolis or to Ohio, where it was sold.

Anna, Russell Regan, and Som Van Cam testified that they drove prostitutes from the Godfather's house to motels.

They stated that they would wait about half an hour, then drive the prostitutes back to the Godfather's house, where the girls would give their money to the Godfather. He would give them crack in return.

Several witnesses characterized Russell as a drug addict who had served as the Godfather's outside security man. Russell was said to have patrolled the property all night. When needed, he also served as a security guard inside the house.

Som was characterized as a security guard, a person that did odd jobs, and a doorman. He had also introduced his friends and relatives to the Godfather, many of whom had subsequently purchased drugs from him.

Robert Morrill, a.k.a. Pallet Bob, had provided security for the Godfather as head doorman. I identified him as the person who had barred my exit from the Godfather's house on March 30, 1995. Pallet Bob said that he had witnessed the Godfather making crack and selling it. Pallet Bob admitted that in July 1995, he had stolen drugs, about $35,000, and other items from the Godfather's house when everyone was at a surprise birthday party for the Godfather at another location.

A few days later the Godfather had confronted Pallet Bob outside an Indianapolis bar and shot him once. The Godfather then pointed the gun at Pallet Bob's head just as a bartender came outside and Pallet Bob was able to get away. Fearing for his life, he had left the state.

Anna testified that later that same evening, the Godfather told her that he had intended to kill Pallet Bob because he had an image to protect.

When Anna was asked what the Godfather would have done to me if he had been convinced that I was a cop, she replied, "He would have shot and killed DeVore!"

It was made abundantly clear that the Godfather was capable of murder. And even after the trial was over, the Page County Sheriff's Office received additional information that the Godfather had admitted to driving to Fort Wayne and shooting to death Wendy Boyd, the prostitute who I drove to the Godfather's house in attempt to buy drugs. In connection with that case, a search warrant for a home in Indianapolis was executed on August 27, 1996. It did not produce the gun or any ammunition, but other articles that were said to be stored with the gun were found.

Various other witnesses testified that the Godfather kept a variety of loaded guns in his house that were to be used for the protection of the drug operation. Pallet Bob said that the Godfather had once told him, "The only good gun is a loaded gun."

Anna confirmed that the Godfather had had a hidden 9mm Smith & Wesson handgun within easy reach when I bought 6.33 grams of crack from them.

Anna also testified that about three weeks prior to their arrests on federal drug charges, the Godfather had transferred property into her name and a lot of cash had disappeared.

The Godfather took the stand in his own defense. He admitted to preparing drugs for Al to help her get out of trouble. But he said he had done so only one time. He said that Al had told him that her boyfriend would stop beating her if the Godfather agreed to prepare the drugs.

"I don't know why I did it. I just did it to help her out, I guess," the Godfather said.

He also said that he had made a living by repairing cars, cleaning up basements, and selling junk at flea markets.

"I tried to take care of all of them," he said, referring to the dozen or so people living in his house and on his property. "I never allowed alcohol or drugs in the house at all. I had no drug dealings at all."

Witnesses for the Godfather's defense described him as a friend and a charitable person who had helped them when they were down. All of them testified that they had never seen any drugs or drugs dealt in his house.

The Godfather's attorney insisted that the Godfather was a victim of circumstance who had been betrayed by disloyal friends and had ended up in the federal criminal justice system by no fault of his own.

"Don't be mesmerized," his attorney told the jury. "They don't have any evidence that he was the mastermind of a drug operation."

During his closing arguments, the federal prosecutor disagreed, portraying the Godfather as a criminal mastermind and accusing him of operating a drug business out of his house under the guise of helping alcoholics, homeless people, and drug addicts.

The six men and six women on the jury were given their instructions and sent out to begin their deliberations. I didn't know how to feel about our chances of a conviction. In a previous federal trial, I had seen a jury return a not guilty verdict in a case that was very solid. Even so, I felt that the Godfather would be found guilty of something. I just didn't know of what.

I tried to keep busy once the jury went out. I hoped that the verdict would bring the closure that I needed and help to ease the anxiety that I had experienced as a result of my meeting with the Godfather more than a year earlier.

The Godfather was facing a minimum of five years in a federal prison. Already the members of his organization had pleaded guilty to various charges and had testified against him. The friendships he might have made during the time of his criminal activities were no longer in existence. The Godfather's common-law wife, Anna Streeter, whose testimony had been the most damaging, was no longer at his side.

The empire he had built – drugs, prostitution, and stolen property – was gone. His yard full of cars and trucks was gone. His highly feared reputation on the street was gone. The only question that remained was for how long he would lose his freedom.

The next day, April 10, 1996, I got word from Stephanie that the jury had reached a verdict. I hurried down to the federal courthouse and rushed inside. I wanted to find Assistant U.S. Attorney Stephen Conley and Agent Turner.

As I turned a corner, I saw both men standing outside the courtroom. They were as anxious as I was. The three of us entered the courtroom together and sat down at the prosecutor's table. The jury and Judge Wolff were not in the courtroom.

Several of the Godfather's friends and family members, including his ex-wife and his daughter, were already seated.

I had an uneasy feeling. What had the jury decided? Was the Godfather going to be found guilty on the drug charges and sentenced to only a couple of years in prison?

Minutes later, three U.S. marshals escorted the Godfather into the courtroom. He was not handcuffed and was wearing the same clothes that he had worn throughout the trial.

His attorney followed him into the courtroom. They sat down at the defense table. The Godfather leaned over and whispered something to his attorney, who nodded.

The Godfather turned toward his friends and relatives and smiled. They appeared to be very nervous.

Next, the court reporter entered the courtroom and took a seat at her machine. The judge was about to enter. The courtroom was silent. I could hear my heart beating.

I started to sweat. My palms were damp. Suddenly, the door to the judge's chambers opened. Judge Wolff entered the courtroom and sat down at the bench. He instructed the bailiff to bring in the jury.

The Godfather glanced at his friends and relatives. There were no more smiles. They were clinging to each other. The Godfather turned back around in his chair to face the jury.

The bailiff opened the courtroom door. Everyone in the courtroom stood up.

The foreman entered first. The other members of the jury followed him. The last person to enter was the alternate jury member. After they had all taken their places in the jury box, the judge instructed everyone to be seated.

"Has the jury reached a decision in the case of the United States versus Robert Porter?" asked Judge Wolff.

"Yes, we have," replied the jury foreman. "And it was unanimous, Your Honor."

I took a deep breath.

The Godfather looked at the jury. He was visibly nervous. He held his hands together tightly in front of him. He glanced at his attorney. The time had come for the verdict to be read.

Guilty. The jury had found the Godfather guilty.

Immediately following the reading of the verdict the United States Department of Justice and the United States Attorney in the Northern District of Indiana released the following statement to the media:

> INDIANAPOLIS – At approximately 3:20 p.m. on April 10, 1996, a federal jury sitting in the case of U.S. vs. Robert Porter returned guilty verdicts on all counts. The jury had begun its deliberations at approximately 2:00 p.m. on April 9. The trial began on April 1st.
>
> The jury found the defendant guilty on eight counts. Count 1 is the crime of continuing criminal enterprise, which carries a statutory penalty of twenty years to life imprisonment. Count 2 is the crime of conspiracy to distribute cocaine, cocaine base, or methamphetamine, which carries a penalty of ten years to life ....
>
> Counts 6, 8, 12, and 13 are crimes of the use or carrying a firearm in the course of drug trafficking. Each has a penalty of 20 years, which must run in addition to any other penalty .... Estimates of quantities of these drugs testified to at trial ranged up to 17 kilograms of crack, 17 kilograms of powder cocaine, and 10 kilograms of methamphetamine .... A 9mm pistol admitted into evidence at trial was identified by various witnesses as the gun used by the defendant to

shoot another person involved in this drug business on July 21, 1995, in Indianapolis .... United States Attorney Daniel B. Cornelius credited the Federal Bureau of Investigation and the Riverside County Sheriff's Office with the successful investigation of this case .... The United States Attorney particularly praised the investigative efforts of a Riverside County Sheriff's deputy who served in an undercover capacity during the investigation, making a purchase of 6.33 grams of crack cocaine from the defendant and others at the defendant's house on March 29, 1995. A tape recording, played during the trial, was made by the undercover deputy during a March 30, 1995, encounter with the defendant. The conversation on the recording was interpreted to demonstrate the defendant threatening the life of the undercover deputy, should the defendant find that the deputy had been "wearing a wire" during the previous day's drug transaction.

On June 28, 1996, the Godfather was sentenced to life plus forty-five years in a federal prison.

The investigation of the Godfather was the biggest and most successful crack cocaine case in the history of the state of Indiana. As a result, the Godfather is spending the rest of his life behind prison walls.

What had the Godfather gained by choosing to be a criminal? Nothing. He had become an identification number, a federal prison inmate existing in a small cell.

The Godfather had lost all of his treasures because of the choices he had made.

Because of Al's choice to come forward, many dangerous people had been taken off the streets. She had not stopped the flow of drugs in the city completely, but she had made a sizable difference in the community she cared for.

She endured numerous threats against her life following the arrest of the Godfather and the members of his organization, making it necessary for the FBI to move her out of the Indianapolis area. She and her husband divorced.

Al remained committed to her newfound Christian faith, however. The last time I spoke with her, she was winning her drug-addiction battle and was doing odd jobs to make ends meet. I found Al to be an example of how people who want to change their lives can be successful. Not only did she provide intelligence information about the Godfather and his organization, she put her life at risk to help right her wrongs. She chose the less traveled road rather than taking the easy way out.

# Chapter 16

Following the conviction of the Godfather, my fear of working undercover subsided. Once again I was able to convince informants to introduce me to their drug dealers. My confidence was back. I wasn't having nightmares anymore. And, I wasn't afraid that I might be accused of being a cop.

But at that same time, my relationship with my wife was deteriorating. While my professional life was at its peak, my personal life was hitting bottom. It hadn't happened overnight. And, I knew that I was partly to blame.

Before my promotion to detective, I had been assigned to the sheriff's office community relations unit. One of my duties was to teach a weekly drug prevention class, D.A.R.E., to elementary age children. Each lesson started with some of the students sharing stories about what they had done during the week.

For me, the most touching stories were told by the students who had spent the weekend with their fathers. I could sense their excitement and see the joy in their faces.

At that time, I was still married to my children's mother. Listening to the students, I felt fortunate that my children did not have to divide their time between two homes. I often told myself that I would never put my children in that same situation.

But because of the choices I made several years later, I had done just that. Now I was in a difficult and frustrating situation as I tried my best to blend my new family.

The biggest adjustment for me was living with Paula's children full-time and only seeing my children five or six times a month. When my children spent the weekend with us, Nate and Joel were always there, which made my children seem like visiting relatives instead of my children.

We did not have the same family bond that we had had when we lived together in the same house and that change in our relationship was very hard for me to accept. More and more, I was experiencing feelings of guilt. It had been my choice to leave their mother and them. I was responsible for not seeing them every day.

Instead, I was tucking someone else's children into bed every night.

And, every night when I told Nate and Joel good night and that I loved them, I was reminded that I was not with my children telling them that very same thing. (As I write this, it brings tears to my eyes.) The lesson that the choices I made affected other people was a hard one for me to learn. And in most cases, there were no "do overs!"

Paula was also experiencing guilt. Her guilt came from taking her sons away from their father. She also felt guilty about taking them away from their cousins and friends.

Truth be told, Paula and I were having a difficult time living with the choices that we had made in order to be together. As much as we both tried to make our relationship work, we were failing miserably.

Twice during the following months, Paula packed up all of her belongings and said she was going to move back to Illinois. Each time, I was able to convince her to stay.

Our marriage environment was not a healthy one, however, and in October 1996, Paula asked me to move out. I agreed and moved into a friend's place. Shortly after, she packed up and moved back to the Chicago area, taking just about everything. I returned home to an empty house, a house with no love and no furniture. I was brokenhearted.

I couldn't stop thinking about Paula. Even when my children were visiting, I felt like something was missing. I couldn't find anything to fill the void in my life that occurred when Paula had moved out.

Even at work, I thought about Paula. And even though my work continued to yield results, I was distracted. Paula was my primary focus; my children and work came second. Over time, the gap between my feelings for Paula and the feelings that I had for my children and my work grew wider. I was losing sight of the things that had meant the most to me.

In December 1996, I reached out to Paula with a phone call and we talked. Subsequent phone calls followed, and I felt some hope that we might get back together. Finally, Paula confessed that she missed me and our relationship.

However, she said that even though she wanted to give our marriage another chance, she would not move back to Indiana. She wasn't willing to uproot her sons again. If our relationship were going to be renewed, I would have to quit my job and move to Illinois.

I was faced with an important decision. When I had first met Paula, I told her that she had to move to Indiana. I insisted that I could not leave my children and my job. Now, the tables were turned. Could I move out of state and only see my children occasionally? Could I leave the job that I had worked so hard to get?

I weighed all of my options. No matter what I did, I would experience a loss. After much deliberation, I decided to move to Illinois. I felt I had to be with Paula, which justified my decision to sacrifice my relationship with my children.

When I told my children and co-workers about my decision, it was obvious that my choice was an unpopular one. But my desire to be with Paula was so strong, I was willing to give up everything to be with her. "I would rather flip hamburgers for a living and be with Paula than spend the rest of my life without her," I said.

In August 1997, I resigned from the Riverside County Sheriff's Office and moved to Illinois. I found a job in the Chicago area selling cars.

Because Paula did not want to live in an apartment, I reluctantly withdrew all of the retirement savings that I had built up during the past eighteen years and we bought a house.

While I told Paula that I would feel more comfortable if we took things slowly so I could adjust to living far away from my children and to a career change, we immediately began remodeling the house to her specifications.

Soon I was homesick. I missed my children terribly. My new job was quite a change from law enforcement. I knew very little about sales, but thought that if I could do undercover work and convince someone that I was a drug dealer and not a cop, I could certainly sell someone a car.

My days off were Tuesdays and Sundays. Once a month, I got a Saturday and Sunday off. On those weekends, I drove to Indiana to see my children. I quickly realized that those two days didn't allow me enough time to enjoy them like I wanted to. I found being away from my children this much was a bigger sacrifice than I had thought it would be.

My salary had dropped from more than $40,000 a year to about $25,000. While Paula had a job as a bank teller, her standard of living now was much lower than when she'd been married to her first husband. During her previous marriage, Paula did not work outside the home, as her ex-husband had made more than $100,000 a year. We constantly argued about money and what to do with what little we had.

Within two months of moving to Illinois, I realized that I had made a mistake. I was miserable. I missed my children and my work as a detective. Paula and I had fallen back into the same unhealthy relationship. It was a struggle for me to get through the day without regretting my decision to leave my children and Indiana.

But I felt I had too much invested in our relationship to let it fail again. With Paula's encouragement, I decided to try counseling.

She joined me for my first visit. The counselor asked Paula straight out, "Do you still want to be in a relationship with Steve?"

Her response stunned me. With a very distant look in her eyes, she said, "I don't know if I do or not."

For the second time in our marriage, Paula was thinking about filing for divorce.

I began to do everything I could to make Paula happy. I continued to meet with the counselor on a weekly basis. Paula decided that it would be best if she met with a different counselor. So we went to counseling separately.

At one point, I thought that if I changed jobs things would be better. So I got a job as a civilian detention officer at the county sheriff's office.

Initially, I was assigned to the midnight shift, which didn't do much for our relationship. Fortunately, I soon received a transfer to the afternoon shift. At that point we were having some great days and some not-so-great days. We found ourselves arguing about nothing. It felt as though we were better at fighting than we were at building a healthy marriage.

Early in July 1998, we talked about moving to a suburb that was closer to her job as she had recently been promoted to manager of a bank in another town. Her new position was a big change from her previous job as a teller at a local bank.

When Paula had worked as a teller locally, she had been close enough to her sons' school that if they had an event, she could leave work to attend it. She was able to get home before her sons got out of school. In contrast, her new job was thirty minutes from home and she found the commute difficult.

Instead of moving, however, Paula brought home divorce papers a few weeks later. I was stunned. Paula had switched from wanting us to move as a family to asking me to move out and end our relationship.

Questions filled my mind. Would I go back to Indiana? What would I do for a living? Where would I live? My retirement money and savings were gone. I was broke and in a daze.

Suddenly I had to find a place to live, and live by myself. I felt an overwhelming sense of anxiety. It was something that I didn't want to do, but I had no other option. I found an apartment about thirty minutes from the home that I shared with Paula. As I drove back to the house to get my things, I realized that I couldn't remember what the apartment looked like.

My first night on my own was extremely difficult. Even though the apartment would be my home for a while, I felt completely out of place. I had lost everything – Paula, my children, my family, my friends, and my job. It was all replaced by loneliness. I lay in bed in total disbelief. How had this happened?

Over the next few days, my mood grew even darker. I realized that I treasured my relationship with Paula more than anything, including my own life. She had become my life.

I couldn't eat. I struggled to fall asleep at night. Thoughts of how much I missed Paula raced through my mind. When I did fall asleep, I would have dreams about being with Paula. When I woke up, I felt the pain of reality. I was in a state of depression.

When I wasn't working, I was sleeping. Even when I was in Indiana visiting my children, I went back to bed as soon as they left for school. I had so many questions and no answers.

Paula had told me that the only way that she could deal with the divorce was to cut off all contact with me. She refused to talk to me on the phone, see me, or write to me. One day, she was the treasure of my life and, the next day, I didn't feel like I had a life.

One day while visiting my children, I told them that I had lost everything. Their response caught me off guard. "You still have us!" they said.

That statement got my attention. I knew that I had to do something, but I was at a loss. I didn't know where to turn or what to do. How could I or would I get out of the mess that I was in?

One night I came home from work and instead of going to bed, I turned on the television, something I hadn't done for a while.

When I was flipping though the channels, I came across a station that was playing Christian music. I started to listen to the words. The music and words did something I had been unable to do for myself: they helped me forget about my troubles. They prompted me to remember a Bible verse, Proverbs 3:5-6: "Trust in the Lord with all your heart and lean not on your own understanding, in all ways acknowledge him, and he will make your paths straight."

I had accepted Jesus as my savior in 1973. Since that time, I had attempted to live my life as a Christian. I was beginning to understand that I was depressed because of the guilt I was feeling as a result of some of the choices I had made.

I had chosen to make my relationship with Paula my treasure in life. Another verse came back to me, Matthew 6:19-21: "Do not store up for yourselves treasures on earth, where moth and rust destroy, and where thieves break in and steal. But store up for yourselves treasures in heaven, where moth and rust do not destroy, and where thieves do not break in and steal. For where your treasure is, there your heart will be also."

In the past, I had read the Bible. I had read what was written, but I didn't understand how it applied to me. Suddenly I was beginning to understand.

I had put all of my faith and hope into a relationship that could be taken away from me in an instant. I had put my relationship with Paula before my relationship with God. That explained why my heart felt so empty.

I got down on my knees and I started to pray. I told God that I didn't understand why I had made the choices that I had. I considered myself a Christian, but I confessed that I had failed. I prayed for a better understanding of what I needed to do to break free from the guilt and how to find peace in my life.

I felt like such a complete failure. I confessed that my so-called Christian way of living did not bring me happiness. I knew then that the only way I could turn my life around was to seek Jesus and that I had to put my faith and hope in God. He would show me the way out of my pain.

I continued to listen to Christian music when I got home from work. Every night, I watched a Christian television network, Trinity Broadcasting Network (TBN). I was also inspired to read the Bible again.

In those ways I received God's messages. Many of my questions were answered. I stopped worrying about my future. In Matthew 7:25-34, God assured me that I didn't have to worry about my life, what I would eat, or what I would wear. He knew what I needed. If I sought Him first, all those things would be given to me as well.

The first thing that I had to learn was how to serve the Lord. The Pharisees had asked Jesus, "What is the greatest commandment?" Jesus had replied in Matthew 22:37 and 39: "Love the Lord your God with all your heart and with all your mind. The second is love your neighbor as yourself."

In addition to the greatest commandment, I needed to learn about love. In Corinthians 13:4-9, Jesus defined love: "Love is patient, love is kind. It does not envy, it does not boast, it is not proud. It is not rude, it is not self-seeking, it is not easily angered, and it keeps no records of wrongs. Love does not delight in evil but rejoices with the truth. It always protects, always trusts, always hopes, always preserves. Love never fails."

I realized why my relationship with Paula had failed. It wasn't a loving relationship. I did not love her the way that Jesus had instructed. I was not kind or patient. I was rude and kept a record of wrongs. I was easily angered and did not trust her.

I read the definition of love over and over again. I realized that I did not have a loving relationship with my children either. I was making the same mistakes with them. It was my biggest problem. I did not love, as Jesus defined it, the people that were the closest to me. I was failing to love my neighbor as myself.

I reflected back on my life. I had rarely experienced happiness. It became clear to me that I had relied on other people to make me happy. As a result, I was frequently disappointed, frustrated, and unsatisfied. Now I was on my own. How and where would I find happiness?

I read Proverbs 16:20: "He that handles a matter wisely shall find good, and whoever trusts in the Lord, happy is he." The answer was right in front of me. I told God that I would put my trust in Him. I prayed for understanding. I wanted to change, and I wanted to learn how to love.

Every day I was reminded by the inmates I worked with that I needed to change. While I wasn't a criminal, I was a sinner. I had disobeyed God's law. My mistakes and bad choices had had devastating consequences, too.

I was not in jail, but I was a prisoner. The consequences of my mistakes followed me everywhere I went. I couldn't escape the guilt, the anxiety, and the loneliness I felt.

While watching TBN, I heard a pastor say that Jesus died on the cross for our sins. All we needed to do was to confess our sins to God and they would be erased forever. If I did what he said, God's grace and forgiveness would set me free. I wouldn't have to carry around the guilt associated with my mistakes any longer.

I attended church in Indiana when I visited my children. The pastor stated in one of his sermons that to repent meant to simply turn the other way. I told God that I would walk away from my sinful desires. I would walk a path toward Him. I had been a Christian before, but only a part-time Christian. I had only followed Jesus's teachings when it was convenient. When it wasn't convenient, I did what I wanted to do or what felt good at the time.

I finally understood why I had made the choices that I did. I had been on the wrong path. I realized that I needed to dedicate my entire life to serving God. I would find happiness by serving God and by loving others according to Jesus's teachings. Over time I grew more patient and kind; I became less rude and slower to anger. Happiness filled my life. My faith and hope grew. I knew what God meant when He said to store up treasures in heaven. Those treasures couldn't be taken away.

My relationships with my children improved. My relationships with my co-workers also improved. I even had better relationships with the inmates that I supervised.

I decided I wanted to live my life so that others could see God working through me. I prayed that other people would see how my life had changed. And by my witness, I hoped that someone else who was making sinful choices would be compelled to turn his or her life over to God.

I prayed that God would use me everyday to teach others and that my story would give them hope. I wanted to tell others about the happiness that I found through a life of serving God instead of serving my own sinful desires.

I chose to live by the words found in Philippians 4:13: "I can do all things through Christ who strengthens me." I had definitely proven that if I tried to get through life by myself, I wouldn't make it.

With God's strength and through constant prayer, I overcame some of my temptations. I stopped worrying about the future. My depression subsided. I found peace. I was forgiven for making bad choices. And I learned to forgive myself.

# Epilogue

On July 12, 1999, I returned to the Riverside County (Indiana) Sheriff's Office as a civilian detention officer. When I had resigned in 1997, I had lost my seniority and my rank as a detective. But during my time away, I had rediscovered my faith. "My best days are yet to come," I told the sheriff during my interview for the position.

At Grace Lutheran Church on December 2, 2000, my children stood with me in front of a very special group of people at the altar. The occasion was my wedding. I was blessed to have found a very special Christian woman to share the rest of my life with. The woman who would become my wife had introduced herself to me after sharing the peace at a Saturday night "come as you are" service earlier in the year.

While I am aware that there will be many bumps along the way, I know that God will be there to comfort me and guide me.

I started writing this story in March 1997. I wanted to tell everyone about my great undercover abilities and how I had brought down the Godfather. After the investigation, the sheriff's office had not awarded me the Medal of Valor or presented me with any other special awards. This book was going to be my way of building up my self-esteem.

But during the writing of this book, I experienced something that I hadn't expected. My life changed. And I realized that the Godfather and I actually had some things in common.

We had both put our treasures in places where they could be taken away. I also realized something else. I hadn't brought the Godfather down. He had done it himself, by his own choices. I, too, was brought down by my choices.

I challenge you to examine your treasures. We all have them. Are yours work, alcohol, drugs, money, material items, the opposite sex, or any number of other temptations? What choices are you making to get them and keep them?

Recently, a group at work pooled their money and purchased several lottery tickets. The payoff was estimated to be about $45 million. My co-workers talked about what they would do with their money. In each case, it was thought that the money would bring happiness.

Needless to say, they did not win the lottery. All they had left were worthless pieces of paper and empty dreams of what they might have bought. I, on the other hand, had already received the greatest prize of all and it wasn't as a result of buying a lottery ticket.

Through God's grace and forgiveness, I have been given a second chance in life. Now is your chance to experience God's grace and forgiveness. The following is the prayer and confession that will change your life; it changed mine!

> God I am a sinner. My choices have not always been the best. I need your help. I believe that Jesus Christ is your son. He came down to earth as your flesh. He died on the cross to take my sins with him to Hell. You raised him from death, so that now I might have life. Jesus, right now I open my heart to you and ask you to come into my life. May my choices be what you would want, and not what I would desire. Thank you for your forgiveness!

If you pray this simple prayer and mean it in your heart, you will build treasures in heaven that no one can destroy or take away.

In January 2002, I finished writing this book. I pray that my story will give you hope.

Peace be with you.

# Acknowledgements

On October 12, 1978, I started my career in law enforcement. This picture was taken shortly after I was hired. I would like to thank the sheriff, now retired, who gave me the chance to become a deputy sheriff.

My first assignment as a deputy sheriff was in the jail division. The sheriff also gave me the opportunity to work in the patrol division; in community relations, where I assisted in the implantation of the Drug Abuse Resistance Education (D.A.R.E.) program; and as an undercover detective assigned to the organized crime unit.

I would like to thank a former co-worker and close Christian friend who served as my mentor throughout my career in the sheriff's office. He has turned in his badge and is now a pastor.

And, I would like to thank my wife for the time she spent editing this book's rough draft. With thoughtfulness and encouragement, she helped me transform my story into a book.